To Doug –
With thanks,
Dena Miller

Library of Congress Number: 2002096391
ISBN: 0-9727199-0-3

Second Edition





This book was printed in the United States of America.

**To order additional copies of this book, contact:**

**Covered Bridge Publishing, L.L.C.**
P.O. Box 1
Sherman, MS 38869
also available at ***Amazon.com***

# SOUTHERN JUSTICE

**By: Dena Miller**

Editor: Joyce Scallorn Cayson

Cover Photo: Doyle Caviness

Cover Design: Royce Cayson

Covered Bridge Publishing L.L.C.

This book is dedicated to Ben, who inspired me more than he knows.

## Foreword

*Southern Justice* is an intriguing and masterfully weaved tale of the lives of two brothers and their families. This twisted tale of life in the South was inspired by an actual event, and I found myself drawn into every page, trying to solve the mystery of Lyn's death.

Somewhere between the gay bars of Key West, Florida and the placid bluegrass country of Lakeland, Kentucky was the answer, but Mark Lake was innocently caught in the middle. His wife killed and his life destroyed, Mark embarks on a journey of intrigue and deceit while Jason Kelley, Lyn's secret lover, comes to grips with reality.

Mark must witness the mysterious twists and turns of Kelley's final judgment, which will ultimately involve the lives of everyone in the Lake family, including wise Papa Sam, who, quite unaware, has discovered the way of *true* southern justice!

Jamie Lance - author - "The Coming: The Bible's Identity of So-Called UFOs"

# Chapter 1

Mark finished his day at the barn by feeding the horses, and the only thing on his mind as he unlocked the door was a nice long shower. The hay that stuck to his hot and sweaty arms was beginning to sting. "Who the hell could that be," he said out loud to the ringing phone. He thought about ignoring it, but when his grandmother's number popped up on his caller id, he answered before she could hang up.

By the tone of her voice, Mark knew immediately that the car wreck was worse than she would say. Terrified of what he would find, Mark ran out the door, jumped in his truck, and was on his way to the scene of the accident. This can't be happening, he thought. Lyn's got to be all right. Please, God. Please let her be all right.

Mark pulled onto the highway and stomped the accelerator. He was determined to run over everything that got in his way and he sped down the road like a runaway horse crazy with fear, intent on reaching his destination.

I'm never gonna get there, he thought. The faster he drove, the more it felt like he was moving in slow motion. "God, get out of the way," he screamed through the windshield at the slow driver in front of him, and he whipped his truck into the other lane to pass, then quickly slammed on his brakes, realizing why the car in front of him was moving so slow.

There it was. Up ahead in the middle of the road. A crowd was gathered and a large man was flagging traffic. Some of the crowd was trying to help, but most of them only wanted to indulge their morbid curiosity. This infuriated Mark as he wheeled off the road and shoved his truck into park. He hit the ground running as fast as his legs would carry him.

"Get out of the way," he shouted, pushing his way through

the curious onlookers. Debris was scattered everywhere. Then he saw it, upside down in the ditch was Lyn's crushed car. And beside the car, a green hospital sheet attempted to conceal her body. Mark started toward the sheet but his dad held him back. Mark fought hysterically to free himself from his father's grip. "Turn me loose," he screamed to no avail. Then he dropped to his knees in a sea of broken glass and sobbed.

No one made a sound. Even the noise of traffic seemed to subside. Now, the only sound was the heartbreaking wails of a young man whose life would never be the same, the bitter screams of a man who'd lost the only woman he'd ever loved.

Mark's mother took his arm and helped him to his feet. "Come on," she said. "We've got to go get the baby. Your daddy will take care of things here. There's nothing you can do." Mark slowly tried to stand, then he took one last look at the covered body that was once his wife. As he leaned on his mother for support and they slowly walked away, Mark noticed that one of Lyn's hands was uncovered, and her blood-soaked hand was still clutching her cell phone. His knees buckled again and he had to stop to steady himself. Had Lyn tried to call him for help, or was she talking to someone else when the accident happened? Mark suddenly felt nauseated, and he hurried away from the crowd to throw up where no one could see.

Gail tried to comfort her son as much as possible as she methodically went through the house making coffee and answering the phone. It was approaching 6 o'clock, and people were coming home from work and hearing about the accident. Now friends and family were arriving to offer words of consolation and regret. It doesn't take long for news to travel in a small town, especially not in Lakeland, Kentucky, a town with about thirty-five hundred people, most of them related, and all of them loving a good rumor. Mark knew in his heart these people meant well, but hell, he didn't even know most of them. They were friends of his parents or grandparents, not his.

Mark's brother Joey was among the first to arrive and the only person Mark cared anything about talking to. The brothers had always been close, which seemed odd to some since their personalities were as opposite as night and day. Joey was a little rough around the edges and was prone to say exactly what was on his mind at any given moment. Mark, on the other hand, was usually quiet and soft-spoken, even shy at times. The biggest thing they had in common was their love of horses. Being raised up on a horse farm may not have been the most exciting life, and it did take a lot of hard work, but it kept the boys close to each other; and, as Gail had hoped, close to home. Mark was hoping that Joey had talked with their dad. He desperately wanted to know what caused Lyn's accident. But the only thing Joey knew was that their dad was on his way home. Joey poured some coffee and they waited.

Now Larry was coming through the door and the boys were sitting at the kitchen table, ready to bombard him with questions. Larry was a big man standing nearly six feet- six, and weighing about two hundred and sixty pounds. Big men seemed to run in the Lake family, and the old folk would say that the Lakes grew their men like they grew their horses, big and strong. Larry was a good-looking man in a very rugged and weathered kind of way, not exactly the person you'd want to meet coming at you in a dark alley, but in spite of his intimidating appearance, he had a very placid temperament. He was known to have a little too much to drink every now and then, even ending up in a few bar room brawls, but somehow his wife Gail always seemed to get him out of whatever kind of trouble he could get in to, keeping the rumors down to a minimum. That is, except when Larry went on a drunken spree and lost most of their money on a sure thing at the horse track. The rumor mill had survived for months on that juicy morsel. But, even then, it was Gail's shrewd investments and cunning business deals that enabled them to remain in the race horse business. Everyone, including Larry, knew she wore the pants in the family.

Actually, Larry slowed down on his drinking and managed to quit gambling by the time Joey and Mark were born. He and Gail took great pride in the home and their two boys. Facing them now, and especially facing Mark, was one of the hardest things he would ever have to do.

The questions his boys were asking were the same ones Larry was still asking himself. "Son, eyewitnesses said Lyn's car didn't seem to be traveling at an excessive rate of speed. There were no other cars involved and Lyn didn't have to swerve to avoid hitting anything in the road," Larry said as he kept his eyes fixed upon the floor and avoided looking Mark directly in the face. The only explanation Larry offered Mark was that Lyn simply lost control of her car and that it flipped five times, the last time throwing her out of the car and onto the highway. And sadly, Larry had been the one to identify Lyn's body, an image he would never be able to get out of his mind.

The house was now infested with people and Mark wasn't in the mood for company. He knew they meant well, but he needed time alone to sort through his confusion. Mark retreated to the den and collapsed on the floor. His eyes fixed upon the ceiling, and a thousand images were racing through his head. Mark then wondered why people bring food when someone dies. He sure as hell wasn't in the mood for a feast. And, although his friends were with him, Mark wanted to remain in his own private world, a safe place where his feelings could remain only his. Nothing could bring him out of his world, until he heard a familiar little voice whisper, "Daddy." Mark looked up to see his tiny daughter Emily with a puzzled look on her face as if to say, what are all these people doing here?

My God, he thought. She's only two years old. How am I going to raise her by myself? This is so unfair. He sat up and pulled her onto his lap. "Daddy," she said with tears in her eyes. "I want my Mommy."

Just then Joey's wife, Laura, burst into the house and was sobbing so hard she couldn't speak. Lyn was her best friend.

They'd gone everywhere and done everything together, sharing each other's dreams and secrets. And from the moment that Mark and Lyn started dating, Laura had shopped with Lyn and shared her innermost feelings. They loved each other so much, they had even shared each other's most expensive outfits. Now what was she going to do without Lyn? Laura ran through the house until she found Gail. Laura desperately wanted Gail to tell her that the horrible news about Lyn was not true, that it was just another vicious rumor, but Gail only shook her head.

Mark took little Emily out of the house. "Sweetie, your mommie has gone to live with the angels. We'll miss her, but we can't be sad." Mark was astonished at how much his daughter seemed to understand as he took Emily through a tour of the stables. He wanted her to see the newest addition to the Lake family, a beautiful mare that was purchased by his brother Joey that very afternoon. "This is Dewey's Dancing Bell, but you can call her Dancer," Mark told Emily. The Lakes were looking forward to raising several champions off this mare. She'd come from a long line of remarkable performers and they expected her to produce offspring with both speed and stamina. Happily, Dancer was due to foal in late December, and Mark already knew what the baby's name would be, Millennium Magic!

Emily shared her father's love for horses. It was in her blood. In fact, she loved horses so much that the family had to watch her closely to keep her from toddling right under one. Even Lyn's greatest fear had been that Emily would get trampled.

Now Mark held his daughter's hand and they walked slowly through the stables. Neither of them said a word, and neither wanted to go back to the house. But there were decisions to be made, and somehow, Mark had to find the strength to make them.

# Chapter 2

It was the day of the funeral and Joey was awakened by the sound of Laura's weeping. He didn't know what to do for her since she'd not eaten or slept since the news of Lyn's death two days ago. Joey took their two children, Bobby, 6 and Zach, 18 months to stay with family friends. He didn't want the kids to see their mother so upset. It might frighten them.

Laura was a very pretty brunette, but she'd always envied Lyn's long blonde hair and gorgeous blue eyes. To Laura, Lyn had it all. She was tall, thin, pretty, and smart, and Laura wanted to be just like her. She never really understood that there was more to life than having the right outfit for the right occasion, or having the greatest figure or the best tan in town. Maybe that's why she and Lyn had gotten along so well. They both seemed to care more about themselves than they did anyone else.

"I've got to go to Mom's," Joey said. "Mark called late last night and I promised I'd go to her house this morning. He wanted to talk to me about something." Laura stared straight ahead. She never acknowledged that Joey had spoken. Somewhere along the line, she had fallen out of love with Joey. In fact, she couldn't even stand the thought of Joey being in the same room with her, let alone touching her.

Maybe she hadn't loved him at all, she thought. Looking back she realized she had gotten pregnant only to make Joey marry her so that she could get away from her parent's constant bickering. Her mother and father were always drinking and fighting, and fighting and drinking. They finally divorced just last year, but she didn't care. She had another family now, her own. She was just surprised that it took so long for her parents to split up.

Joey Lake, eldest son of Larry and Gail Lake, seemed to

have everything Laura Becker was looking for. He was tall, dark, and handsome. He was smart. He came from a well to do family. And he wanted her. So Laura was grateful that it had only taken three months for her to get pregnant and clinch the deal. Then Gail insisted that she and Joey's dad pay for a big wedding, which was exactly what Laura had been counting on. Within six months, Laura had her new house, a swimming pool in the back yard, and a brand new Corvette. Laura had manipulation down to an art form. And no matter what the circumstances, Laura always got what Laura wanted. That is, until now. And all she wanted now was to have her best friend, Lyn, back.

Joey found Mark out at the stables. Like father, like sons. All three enjoyed spending time at the stables, and whenever one of them had something on their mind, the stables was where they seemed to find comfort. "What's up?" asked Joey. "What do you need to talk to me about?"

"Well," Mark started, then cleared his throat and started again. "I had to go through some of Lyn's things yesterday and I found a letter." He paused, waiting on Joey's reaction. But, Joey did not know where Mark was headed with this conversation. "I found a love letter, Joey, and it wasn't written to me."

"Oh," was all his brother could say. Joey listened as Mark told him of the deceit he'd uncovered and how humiliated and betrayed he felt.

"I was shocked when I found Lyn's letter, but to tell you the truth, I'm not really surprised. We'd been arguing a lot since Emily was born. And during that time, I was finding receipts for purchases of men's items, but the prices were always burned off. And a few months ago, I found a phone bill with a missing page. It was the page that listed all the numbers that were called. I questioned Lyn about the missing page, but after I did, I never found another phone bill again. And nothing could justify the large number of miles being put on her car. You see, Joey, sex had been nonexistent, no matter what I tried. No matter what

I'd confronted Lyn with, she always seemed to lie her way out of it. If lying didn't work, she'd rant and rave and throw things at me, until she'd take whatever I had accused her of and turn it around on me. And then at other times, she would conveniently get sick to avoid me."

Lyn had been diagnosed with bulimia in high school and she'd learned how to make herself throw up whenever she deemed it necessary. Mark knew better than to believe her, but he wanted to. He loved his wife, daughter, and his home. He wanted to believe that things were as good as they'd once been. So he overlooked Lyn's mood swings, her lies, and her not wanting to be touched. He just kept pressing forward with the hope that she would get everything out of her system and settle back down with him again.

Joey soaked up everything he heard. He had no trouble believing what Mark was telling him. In fact, he'd had his suspicions. "Does anyone else know about the letter?" he finally asked.

"You're the only one I've told," Mark said. "If anyone else knows, it's because Lyn told them." Mark and Joey both suspected that Laura knew just about everything there was to know but neither one of them spoke it.

"Do you know who the letter was intended for?" Joey asked.

"I know exactly who it was for. Jason Kelley, that bastard she worked for. She spent too many weekends at the office lately. And too many nights he has called my house to supposedly ask her things about work." Mark's grief had turned to anger and he grew madder and madder just thinking about Kelley touching his wife.

"Okay man, just calm down," urged Joey. "Just calm down and try to think what to do."

"What to do? The man destroyed my life. She was on her way to see that bastard when she died."

"How do you know that?"

"I know that because Lyn called Mom and asked her to pick

up Emily from the day care, telling her that she had to go back to the office to work late. And Joey, I think she was talking to him on the phone when she lost control of the car. Once I get the phone bill, I'll know for sure."

Mentally, Mark buried Lyn that moment he first discovered her letter to Jason Kelley. And now, it was time to bury her again. The whole town of Lakeland turned out for her funeral in the little country church where the Lake children had grown up. The church was so packed, some people had to stand outside. But the amazing thing to Mark was the number of single women that showed up. Lyn's obituary should actually have read: "single white male seeks single white female for sex and companionship", because Mark had just become the most eligible bachelor in Lakeland.

Mark Lake was as tall and good-looking as his brother Joey. But that's where their similarities stopped. Joey had jet-black hair and dark brown eyes, just like his father, Larry. But Mark's hair was blonde and his eyes were ice blue. They were even bluer when he had a dark tan and wore his dark blue suit. Now, all eyes were on Mark as he walked through the crowd to take his place on the front row.

All of Lyn's high school classmates, and some of the girls she worked with were present. Mark wondered what these girls knew as he walked by. Also attending were family members that were so distant, Mark didn't know them. There was, however, one face that did not appear in the crowd. Joey made sure that Lyn's boss did not attend the funeral. He knew the right people to call to make sure that the message got delivered.

Mark sat silently wishing he could have seen Lyn just one more time, to ask her why. Didn't he try to give her everything she ever wanted? While the minister spoke, Mark slipped into his own world. He had gotten good at leaving the scene when it got to be more than he could handle.

Katherine Lyndia Thompson Lake, born January 20, 1976,

went to be with her Lord and Savior on July 10, 1999. Reverend George kept the sermon short and after listing Lyn's survivors, closed with a prayer. The choir sang Amazing Grace as everyone was herded out the back of the church by the funeral director. Mark went through the motions as he was directed to the cemetery. And as the town gathered to lay Lyn's body to rest, the wind began to blow and rain clouds started to form. It's always stormy when somebody dies, he thought.

After the graveside services were complete, Reverend George shook Mark's hand and offered up some words of comfort. Many of the people filed by Mark to wish him well, some telling him to call if there was anything they could do. A few of the girls even slipped him a phone number just in case he might need it. Mark noticed one girl that hadn't said anything to him. She looked vaguely familiar but he couldn't place her. He moved over by his dad and whispered, "You know, I wish people would at least get my damn name right and stop calling me Joey."

Mark walked with his parents to greet family members that he did know and to thank his friends and cousins for being pallbearers. Joey helped Laura, who was still wailing, to the car. When he was sure he was out of hearing range he grabbed her arm, looked her straight in the eye and said, "I know it's Lyn's little secret that's kept you from sleeping at night. But what I don't know is how many of your secrets did she carry to that grave with her?" She snatched her arm out of Joey's grasp and turned to look out the window. They did not speak again until they arrived home.

"Shut up," Joey screamed as he got out of the car. "You're gonna have to get a grip on yourself. You'll find someone else to spend money with." Laura sneered at him as she walked through the door he'd graciously unlocked for her. She went straight upstairs to change clothes. Joey yanked off his tie and grabbed the remote control while he screamed up the stairs, "Are you going to get the kids or am I?"

Ten minutes had passed before Laura came downstairs with

purse in hand. "I am," she said as she walked out the door.

This heartbreak had really taken a toll on Larry's aging parents. Sam turned eighty-two in the spring and Martha was just a few years behind. Papa Sam, as his grandchildren called him, had come back to Lakeland after World War II and started breaking horses to work the fields on his father's farm. It's said among the townspeople that there wasn't anything Sam Lake couldn't get a horse to do.

Other than that, he'd built a reputation of integrity. The whole town, which of course had been named after his ancestors, liked him very much and knew he was a man of his word. But, it wasn't long until machines were replacing workhorses, so he took what little money he had saved and ventured into the world of thoroughbreds. He'd never regretted it. Horseracing had become a huge business in Kentucky and Sam Lake was recognized throughout the south as having one of the most successful breeding facilities in the industry. His ranch had produced more Derby winners than any other ranch in Kentucky and two of those champions walked away with the Triple Crown.

When Sam met Martha Hardin, he thought she was the most beautiful thing he'd ever laid eyes on. A true southern belle he called her, with long brown hair and big dark eyes. She had spunk too, but when Sam learned of her love for horses, he knew she was the woman for him.

"There was no such thing as long engagements in those days," Martha would say. They married quickly and had five children: Sam Jr., Phillip, Larry, Michael, and Elizabeth, their only girl. Even though her long brown hair had been gray for many years, Martha would still laugh and say, "It's a good thing Sam finally got that girl he wanted, or I'd still be having babies."

She had an infectious sense of humor and could tell the most interesting stories. She loved to tell of their rags to riches life and how some of their best times were when the only thing they had was each other. Even though the years had slowed her physically, she had not lost one ounce of her wit. And even more incredible, she had the ability to take a bad situation and somehow make it seem not so bad. She could find something good in everything and everyone.

Sam and Martha Lake had built their home just a few miles out of town, and with several thousand acres of farm and pasture land, had promised each one of their five children enough land to settle on. But all of their children, except Larry, wanted to seek their fortune elsewhere. Oh, they understood when each child left for this or that reason, but they were elated when Larry wanted to learn the family business. They were also thrilled that The Blue Ridge Ranch would carry on, even after they were gone. They were even more thrilled that Mark and Joey wanted to stay right there in Lakeland. They loved having their grandchildren and great grandchildren so close, especially now that Lyn was gone. Mark needed his family near; he needed their support and he needed their help with Emily.

At least half of the people at the funeral showed up back at Sam and Martha's house to continue visiting. Sam, Jr. and Phillip left immediately for the airport in Lexington. They were partners in a computer software company in Dallas and had commitments that had to be met. Martha loved to have all of her children back in the nest, but she understood better than anyone did about the sacrifices necessary to succeed in business. Michael, along with his wife and children would stay the night and head back to Louisiana in the morning. After graduating Kentucky State University with a degree in Petroleum Engineering, he'd landed a job with an oil company and was working his way up the corporate ladder. Elizabeth, who had not yet married, was teaching gifted children at a high school in Louisville and working on her master's degree. She was on summer break and decided to stay a few days to be with her parents.

It had been an unusually hot summer, and the heat had drained the energy from Sam's body. His back was injured many years ago when a stallion he was riding took a tumble and rolled over on top of him. As a result, Sam developed a degenerative disc disease, which gradually worsened over the years. He'd learned to live with the constant pain, but had to rely on a walking cane to keep his balance. He was tired now and had to rest a while. Not to mention that his heart was breaking to see his grandson, Mark, hurting this way. "I don't know why anybody in their right mind would give up clean air and blue skies for smog and traffic," he grumbled. "That's just horseshit," his favorite expression. Then Sam disappeared into the bedroom.

Elizabeth helped her mother and aunts set out the pies, cakes, and the other goodies that friends and neighbors were kind enough to bring over. There was enough food to feed a small army. Elizabeth fixed herself a cup of coffee and made her way to the back porch where she found Larry by himself. "Can I get you anything?" Elizabeth asked.

"No," he said. "I'm not hungry."

"Where'd Gail and Mark go after the funeral?"

"Gail has gone to pick up Emily, and Mark is out at the stables. He needs some time alone."

"That Emily sure looks an awfully lot like her mother," Elizabeth said.

"It's the eyes," Larry replied. "She has Lyn's eyes. But, I think she's going to be built like her daddy."

"She'll be three soon, won't she?" Elizabeth asked.

"Yea, and she's already a little chatterbox."

"You know, Larry. No matter how hot it gets, there's always a cool breeze blowing on this back porch."

"Yea. I think it'll be raining by tonight, though. The clouds are getting pretty heavy looking."

# Chapter 3

Lyn had seen her mother and father go through a very bitter divorce when she was only three. And although she didn't remember a lot about her father, her mother made sure that her memories of him were not good ones. She never felt loved by her father, and her mother was so busy looking for husband number two that she never had much time for Lyn. By the time she'd reached the seventh grade, she was suffering from depression. Feelings of loneliness and despair haunted her, and she gained weight, as a lot of girls do at that age. But by the eighth grade, she was making herself throw-up after she'd eaten. Lyn was also into drinking, because alcohol made her happy, she thought. And beer was so easy to get. She would ask one of the older guys to buy her a six pack. And they always would, that is, as long as she'd buy them one too.

Lyn's body took on a more grown-up shape during the summer after eighth grade, and by the time she went back to school in the fall she'd matured into a gorgeous creature that every guy at Lakeland High School wanted to date. Lyn was elected cheerleader. After that, she started making new friends and her popularity soared. Lyn turned heads everywhere she went, and she was invited to all the right parties. But Lyn had another side. She'd also gotten good at hiding that insecure little fat girl that she believed herself to be on the inside. She appeared happy and carefree to most, but when she looked in the mirror, she still saw an ugly little girl that no one wanted. Lyn could be described in one sad statement. She wanted to be loved.

Mark and Lyn started dating at the beginning of their sophomore year when Mark was attending a party, and there she was, the most beautiful girl he'd ever seen. "Hi, I'm Mark Lake. What's your name?"

"I'm Lyn Thompson," she replied as she staggered closer to the bonfire. "Hey, Mark, would you bring me another beer?"

"Hold on there," Mark said as he grabbed Lyn's arm, pulling her away from the fire. "You know Lyn, I don't think you need anything else to drink. Let me take you home."

Lyn never had anyone treat her as nice as Mark, and she felt a closeness with him, one that she'd never felt with anyone before. Mark made her feel like she was worth something. Now she doted on him, and Mark, well, Mark loved being doted on. They became inseparable. When Mark introduced her to his family, she loved them all, because they, too, made her feel as if she belonged. The whole time she was growing up she had yearned to be a part of a real family and she desperately wanted to be a part of this one.

As graduation approached, Mark struggled with the decision of whether to go to college or not. Most of his friends knew what they wanted to do with their lives and it seemed to Mark that everyone had a sense of direction except him. Lyn was no help. She wasn't going to decide anything until Mark made up his mind. Her goal had already been defined. She was going to become Mrs. Mark Lake and that was the only career she needed.

Graduation came and went and Mark was still undecided about his future. He was spending more and more time at the stables and less and less time with Lyn. She'd taken a part-time job in a day care for the summer, which gave her a little spending money but kept her from having to commit too much of herself while she waited on Mark to make up his mind. But by mid-summer, Lyn was growing impatient. She was tired of Mark's procrastinating. And for the life of her, she could not figure out what was so fascinating about those damned horses. To hell with playing it cool, she thought. It's time to make something happen whether he's ready or not.

Mark was hoping that Joey didn't want to give Prince's Paradise to Bobby. He kind of wanted her himself. Paradise was never going to run again, but she was good for several more babies. He brushed through her mane one last time, and as he reached for her blanket, he saw Lyn coming down the corridor. "What are you doing?" she asked.

"Oh, just trying to get to know Paradise a little better. What are you doing here in the middle of the day?"

"Well, I missed you. We haven't seen much of each other lately and I wondered if anything was wrong."

"No," Mark said. "Nothin' is wrong. I just have a lot on my mind. I come out here to the stables to think about things. It helps me to clear my head."

Lyn moved closer to Mark. "What can I do to help?" she asked. But, before he could answer her, she reached up to kiss him. Her kiss was different from what Mark had been used to. It was more passionate, almost as if she were on fire. And he grabbed her around her tiny waist and pulled her body next to his. Lyn had never before given herself to Mark, but now the time was right. Maybe this would help him make up his mind.

Mark moved his hand under Lyn's shirt and unhooked her bra. This is where she usually stopped him, he thought. His hand touched her breast and he moved his mouth down her neck until he touched her other breast with his tongue. He jerked her shirt off, throwing it to the side, picked her up and carried her into the tack room. He ripped the blankets off their racks and threw them on the floor. Then he gently laid her on them. She slid out of her jeans as he got out of his, and then he was on top of her. There was no stopping now. He pushed himself inside her. "I love you Mark," she moaned as two bodies became one.

"I love you too, Lyn."

A few more weeks passed and if Mark was going to go to school he had to make a decision soon. He spent some time researching Kentucky State and finally decided to go there, if for no other reason his friends would all be there. He still didn't know what he wanted to do, but thought he'd go ahead and get all of his core courses out of the way. Maybe, he hoped, being in a campus environment would inspire him. His parents would support him no matter what he did, but the hard part was going to be telling Lyn. They had a date on Friday night, he remembered. That's when he'd tell her.

Mark was in a wonderful mood as he turned into Lyn's driveway. He felt like the weight of the world had been lifted off his shoulders since he'd finally decided what to do about school. He was just hoping that Lyn would feel as good about this as he did. He could see that Lyn's mother was not home from work and he was glad. There was something about her he really didn't like, although her dad seemed nice. But he'd never been able to pinpoint why Lyn didn't want to have anything to do with him. Mark parked his car and hopped out.

When he got to the door, he could hear Lyn screaming from her bedroom. "I'll be out in a minute," she said. "I'm not quite ready." Mark flipped on the TV, knowing that Lyn's minute would be at least thirty.

At last, she had every hair in place and her makeup just perfect. "Where would you like to go tonight?" Mark asked her as they walked out the door.

"I don't know," Lyn said. "What do you want to do?"

"Well, actually, I'd like to go some place where we could talk. If that's okay with you?" They decided to have dinner at their favorite Chinese restaurant, then they drove to the park.

They sat and looked at the stars for the longest time, making small talk about this and that. Finally, Mark told Lyn he'd made up his mind to move to Lexington in the fall with his friends. "What?" she scowled. "I thought you'd decided to stay here with me."

"We'll still be able to see each other," he said. "I'll come home every weekend or you can come to Lexington to see me. I've told some of the guys I'd share an apartment with them instead of moving into a dorm."

"Why didn't you tell me sooner? Did you think you would

just wait until the last minute to drop this bomb on me?"

"I didn't tell you sooner because I didn't know myself. I've given this a lot of thought and I really believe I've made the right choice."

"Well," Lyn sneered. "Did you even once consider where we stood while making your decision?"

Mark found himself becoming more and more defensive. "I should have known better than to think you'd give a damn what was best for me right now. All you think about is yourself, and yes, I did consider where we stood when I made this decision. And what I discovered is I'm not ready to make that kind of commitment yet. I don't want us to end up like Joey and Laura. They're miserable and I don't want to spend my life miserable. When I make that kind of commitment, I want to be sure."

"You didn't seem very miserable that day in the tack room," she spat.

"Oh I get it," he said shaking his head. "Well, it didn't work. Why can't you understand? Why can't you see that I need more time?"

"Because," she said. "I love you. I thought you loved me too. I just don't think I can stand it with you off in Lexington without me."

"You don't trust me," came his retort. "Well, if we can't trust each other, maybe we don't need to keep hanging on to this relationship anyway."

"Fine," she said. "If that's the way you want it, and obviously it is. Take me home."

"Fine," he echoed. Mark drove Lyn home, neither one saying a word.

Mark was excited to arrive in Lexington. He was the last one of four guys to get moved in. He hadn't finished unpacking when two of his roommates burst into his room screaming, "Party on frat row tonight man. We got to be there." This was a different world for Mark and he was going to like it. It had been years since he'd been to a party without Lyn and he wondered how strange it would be.

"I'll be there," he shouted. "Wild horses couldn't keep me away."

Lyn and Laura had grown close during the past couple of years and Laura had no intention of ending her friendship just because Mark and Lyn's relationship was over. Although, since the breakup all Lyn had done was grieve. Laura tried to comfort her, running to Lyn's house every time she called. But, even she was beginning to think Lyn was about to go over the edge.

"You've got to get a grip on yourself," Laura told her one night. "Stop moping around this house all of the time and get out and have some fun."

Lyn's drinking was getting worse again too. "Without Mark," she cried; "I have no reason to live. He's everything to me."

"Then call him," Laura said. "Call him up and tell him how you feel. At least you'll be doing something besides sitting around here drinking."

Mark answered the phone on the fourth ring. He didn't want to appear too anxious in case it was Lyn. He missed her. She was the only girl he'd ever dated seriously. The last memory he had of her was when she slammed the car door and ran into her house on the night he told her that he was moving to Lexington. He'd relived that night many times.

"Is that you Mark?" she sobbed into the phone.

"Yes, baby, it's me."

"Oh Mark. I'm so sorry. Please forgive me. Please take me back, Mark. I can't live without you. I'll kill myself if you won't take me back."

He could tell she was drinking, but he couldn't tell how much. "I need you, Mark. I need you here with me," Lyn cried into the phone.

"OK, babe, I'll be there in a few hours." Mark was off to Lakeland. But when he arrived and knocked on Lyn's door, he couldn't believe the way she looked. Her hair was a mess, she wore no make-up, and her eyes were swollen and red.

"Oh baby," she snubbed. "I'm so glad you came. I'm so sorry I couldn't understand about school, but I do now. I understand now and I'll wait for you as long as it takes because I love you Mark. I'll do whatever you want me to as long as you'll take me back. I need you Mark. I need you and I've missed you."

"I've missed you too," Mark replied.

For the next few months, Mark spent his weeks at school in Lexington and his weekends at home in Lakeland. Lyn was taking an interest in the horses and wanted Mark to teach her how to ride. They were getting along great, but his grades were suffering. The week of finals rolled around and Mark explained to Lyn that he would have to stay at school over the weekend so he could study, but that he would make it up to her during Christmas break. He had to do well on his final exams or he was not going to pass four out of five of his subjects.

Mark came in late from the library and checked the front of the refrigerator for messages. He saw that Lyn had called so he grabbed a beer and sat down in front of the TV to call her back. "Hey babe. How ya doin'?" he asked when she answered the phone.

"Don't hey babe me! Where the hell have you been?" she screeched back at him.

"Calm down," he said. "I've been at the library studying."

"And just who have you been studying?" she demanded to know.

"What is the matter with you, Lyn? I told you I was staying at school this weekend to study and that is exactly what I have been doing."

"Are you sure there isn't someone else?"

"There is no one else. I promise. Now if that's all you need to know, I've got to get some sleep so I can get up and do it all over again tomorrow."

"All right. I love you, Mark."

"I love you, too. Good night."

"Have you decided what you'd like to do with the rest of you life, son?" Gail asked. Mark still didn't have a clue, but he was glad to have Christmas break to think about it. It was hard trying to juggle school and Lyn. She was very demanding he confided to his mom.

"Well, she didn't have much of an example set for her," Gail said, and then changed the subject. "You know there's always room for you here at Blue Ridge should you change your mind. But, we'll support you whatever you decide."

"Thanks Mom. The ranch becomes more appealing to me all of the time."

Mark received his grades on Christmas Eve and Christmas morning gave Lyn and his mother the Christmas present they were wanting. He was not going back to school. Instead, he would stay at the Blue Ridge Ranch and work with Joey and his dad. He had another surprise for everyone too. After all the other presents were opened, Mark handed Lyn a small package he had hidden under the tree. Her heart stood still. Slowly and carefully she tore the paper off and opened the box to find the diamond ring she'd been waiting for all of her life.

"Life just doesn't get any better than this," Mark told Joey as they drove home from the bar. They'd stopped for a cold one on the way back from the feed store. "I've got a beautiful wife, a beautiful home, and a brand new baby girl. I'm even able to work at doing what I love. What more could a man want?"

Joey knew better than to buy off on Mark's happiness. Laura had told him that Mark and Lyn were not getting along very well since Emily had been born. Lyn had a rough pregnancy and a very difficult labor. Since she'd been home from the hospital she'd been really depressed. "Laura says that Lyn's having a hard time getting over having Emily," Joey said. "You wanna tell me about it or just sit there and pretend the problem doesn't exist?"

"I'd like to just sit here and pretend it doesn't exist but that's not gonna help anything. I don't know if it's that hormone thing or what it is. She'll be doing fine one minute and the next minute she's exploding into someone I don't even know. She's always been a high spirited little filly, but lately I never know what I'll find when I get home."

"What do you mean? Is Emily being neglected?"

"Oh no," Mark replied. "Lyn's a good mother. She doesn't begrudge Emily for feeling the way she does. She blames all that on me. I've tried to get her to see if the doctor can give her something to help get her through this, but so far, she hasn't talked to him about it."

Lyn knew she'd better take a shower while the baby slept. Emily would be awake soon and Mark would be home. They would probably both be hungry. She didn't have much of an appetite herself. She had crash dieted after Emily was born and was now back to her usual twenty pounds under weight. She looked in the mirror and felt ashamed for the way she had treated Mark. No matter what he did, it irritated her. Nothing made her happy anymore. She used to love making love with Mark and now she couldn't stand the thought of him touching her. "What is the matter with me?" she asked the reflection in the mirror. "Am I going insane?"

"I hate living this close to your parents," Lyn told Mark when he came through the door. "Your mother is always trying to run our business. I'd just gotten out of the shower and before I could even dress, your mother is calling wanting to know why I haven't brought Emily over lately. She was asking me all kinds of questions. She's cooked supper for everyone and wants us to come eat. I'm telling you now, Mark, just because Laura always does exactly what Gail says doesn't mean I'm going to."

"She's just concerned about you," Mark said. "She knows you haven't been yourself lately."

"The only thing your mother is concerned with is whether or not she's going to be able to control you and I the same way she controls Joey and Laura. You go. And take the baby with you. I could use some time alone."

Mark went to his parents and took Emily with him. He made the usual excuses that Lyn wasn't feeling well, and when he got back home later that evening, Lyn's anger had been replaced by self-pity. "How are you feeling?" Mark asked her.

"Useless," she answered. "There's nothing to do around here. I'm bored and I feel like I've been cut off from the outside world. How would you feel about me getting a job? Emily is old enough to stay at the day care now, or your mother or grandmother might want to keep her."

"I thought you didn't want my family knowing our business."

"Well, they're always complaining that they don't see enough of her."

"If getting a job is what it would take to make you happy, then by all means Lyn, get a job."

Lyn was now working for the law firm of Thaxton, Sims and Kelley, mostly answering the phones and taking messages, but she felt significant. She got along with the other girls in the office at first, but after a couple of months, that seemed to change. "They're just jealous," she told Laura one day. "After all, Mr. Kelley does pay more attention to me."

Jason Kelley was a very handsome man. He was in his early thirties with a wife, Adriane, and two young children, although you'd never know he was married from the way he behaved around the office. He was a real ladies man, always trying to attract the attention of every woman in the room. And he'd made sure to interview and hire Lyn while both Mr. Thaxton and Mr. Sims had to be in court. At first, his flirtatious ways made Lyn uncomfortable, but she soon began to enjoy his little advancements. He had a charming air about him that Lyn found fascinating. And above all else, he made her feel good about herself. She felt attractive and desirable, the way she'd felt the night she first met Mark.

# Chapter 4

The rain was falling so hard, Mark couldn't see the road in front of him. He slowed the truck to a snail's pace and turned up the radio. The weatherman was predicting more rain and warning people that some of the smaller creeks and rivers would begin to overflow their banks by morning, but Mark knew that the ranch was in no danger. The Lake property was located southwest of Lexington in the Bluegrass Region, one of the most beautiful areas in the state. When you turned up the road leading to the Lake's, the first thing you'd see would be acres and acres of white fencing and bluegrass. Actually, the grass was really green, but it had buds with a purplish-blue tint, which made the pastures look blue from a distance.

Lyn had been gone now for two weeks, and it had rained ever since. This night was no different from the past several. Mark stayed in the stables until after dark, then headed for the bar where he drank until Marty just wouldn't sell him anymore. Marty's Place was the local watering hole just outside of town and Marty, an old friend of Larry's, had always made it a point to watch out for Joey and Mark. Marty played football with Larry in high school and they'd done their share of drinking and running around. So it was a natural thing to keep an eye out for each other's boys.

Mark was terribly depressed and found himself wondering ironically if this was the way Lyn had felt. He was tired too. He hadn't slept an entire night since the accident. Since the funeral, he and Emily had been staying at Larry and Gail's, but it was time to go home. Mark knew he needed to pull himself together; he had to get used to the idea of being alone. Most of all, he had to get himself together for Emily. She had already lost one parent.

Against his mother's will, Mark took Emily home that night. They played and read stories until she fell asleep in his arms. It was odd to him how quiet things were. The sound of the rain falling outside was all he could hear and somehow it was soothing to him. He considered going back to school, but quickly remembered that school would be time taken away from Emily.

In some ways he was scared. And in a weird kind of way, he was relieved. Experience had indeed been a good teacher. He no longer asked himself why Lyn had married him, but he was now questioning why he had married her. As he looked down at Emily, he realized just how much she looked like her mother. This little person was the greatest thing that had ever happened to him. She needed him and he wasn't about to let her down. Mark cried. Then he slept.

During the next week, the rain finally stopped. Mark started mending fences, and he and Emily slowly began to define "normal life" again. Mark put Emily back into day care, so she could develop a routine again. He also had a few friends that would stop by occasionally to keep him company, and his brother Joey was hanging real close. Every day seemed to get a little better, until the day the phone bill came.

Mark opened the bill for Lyn's cell phone and flipped to the page of itemized calls. He immediately found July 10th and followed the listing down until he saw 4:36 PM, the time of her last call. Then, his eyes moved across the page to the phone number. She hadn't been calling for him, but he recognized the number she'd called. Still, just to be sure, he went to the kitchen and opened the drawer where he kept the phone book. He turned to the listing of Thaxton, Sims, and Kelley. And there it was, in bold print, the same number, Lyn's last call. Lyn had been calling Kelley to confirm their plans. Mark knew this now, because Lyn's previous call had been to Gail, asking her to pick up Emily from day care. She then called Kelley to confirm their plans. Now the last missing piece of the puzzle fell into place, just as

Mark suspected. Mark unlocked the liquor cabinet and found a new bottle of Kentucky's finest bourbon. He opened it and threw the top across the room, cranked the stereo as loud as it would go, then took a drink.

"Larry," Gail yelled as she ran into the barn and saw Larry with one of the training jockeys. "You've got to go check on Mark," she said breathlessly.

"What's wrong?" Larry asked.

"I don't know, but I can see a fire from my kitchen window and when I walked outside I could hear the music blaring so loud it sounds like he's having a party over there. I tried to call him, but there was no answer. He probably couldn't hear the phone ring. I'll go pick up Emily; you just go make sure he's all right."

Joey pulled into Mark's driveway right behind Larry. He too had heard the noise and wondered what was going on. Mark had a huge fire in his backyard and he was busy carrying armloads of Lyn's clothes from the closet and throwing them into the fire. He paid no attention to Larry when he tried to stop him.

"Don't interfere, Dad," said Joey. "Mark's drunk and you'd better not get in his way."

"There's no sense in doing this," Larry told his son.

"You don't understand Dad, just leave him alone."

Larry backed off and watched as his son burned every shred of evidence that reminded him that a Lyn had ever lived in his house. And when every article that reminded him of Lyn was gone, Mark pulled a chair to the fireside and sat down. Joey and Larry followed suit as Mark picked up the bottle of bourbon that was almost empty and finished it off.

Joey took it upon himself to get another bottle from underneath the seat in his truck. He handed it to Mark and asked, "You got the phone bill today, didn't you?"

"Yea, I got the phone bill today. It only proved what I already knew." He took a drink from the fresh bottle and lit a cigarette. "Dad," he slurred. "I think there's something you need to know."

Mark's words kept running together, but somehow he managed to relive every last detail of his unhappy marriage. The shocking truth began to unfold as he told Larry about all his suspicions of Lyn, with Joey filling in for him during his drunken pauses. Mark rambled on for two hours, and by the time he'd revealed how he'd finally uncovered the truth, Joey and their dad were about as bombed as he was. "Any more whiskey?" Larry wanted to know.

"There is at my house," shouted Joey. "I'll be right back." He jumped up and made for his truck again.

"I kept thinking she'd get Jason Kelley out of her system, Dad," said Mark. "I just kept hoping she'd get over him and settle back down with me. She wasn't a bad person and I don't want you to hate her. She was just messed up. I kept trying to give her everything she wanted, but looking back, I don't think she even knew what it was that would make her happy. She searched all of her life for something she couldn't even identify and she died without ever figuring it out. All I can hope for is that she's in a place where it doesn't matter anymore. I hope she's finally found some peace." Mark looked over at his dad to see a tear trickle down his cheek and drip off his jaw. Then he looked away quickly so Larry would not know he had seen.

The two men sat silently gazing into the fire until Joey wheeled back into the yard and broke their gloominess. He jumped out of his truck and started towards them when he lost his balance and staggered right into the side of the truck. He bounced back and staggered left for a minute. Then he stopped, spouted a few obscenities, and tried to go forward again. Larry and Mark started snickering. Joey was laughing too, which made walking so much harder. Finally Joey dropped to his knees and crawled back to the fire, carefully protecting the bottle in his hand. The three of them laughed until they cried. It was great therapy.

"What the hell are you boys doing?" Sam asked as he walked up.

Larry jumped like a kid caught with his hand in the cookie jar when he heard his father's voice behind him. "Pull up a bucket or somethin' and join us," Larry garbled, trying to regain his composure. Joey handed Sam the bottle of whiskey he'd just retrieved and Mark filled him in on the details.

He finished his story then added, "You know Papa Sam; I think God finally just had enough of the horseshit and decided to put his foot down."

"Horseshit is right," Joey slurred, his words running together. "That bastard, Jason Kelley, better be watchin' his back around Lakeland. I'm gonna . . . "

"You ain't gonna do nothin'," Mark interrupted. "I'll be takin' care of him myself."

Sam took a drink of the bourbon, then put the top on the bottle and shoved it down into his boot. "You boys don't need anymore of this," he said standing up. "Just don't get in a big hurry to do anything, Mark. These things usually have a way of taking care of themselves, if given a little time."

"I'm starvin'," Joey said rubbing his stomach. "Ain't yawl hungry?"

"I could eat somethin'," replied Mark, wanting to argue with Papa Sam, but knowing better.

"I bet your mother's got something fixed for supper," Larry said. "There'll be plenty, Dad. Why don't you come eat with us?"

"You boys go ahead," Sam said picking up his walking cane. "I've already eaten." Sam tottered toward his truck then turned to look at Mark, "Where did you say this Kelley fella is?"

"Joey said he'd heard he's been in the hospital in Lexington with heart problems ever since Lyn's accident. Why?"

"No reason," said Sam. "But, I think it'd be best if we kept all of this to ourselves for right now. Okay boys?"

"Okay Pop," everyone agreed.

"You boys better go get yourself something to eat now. I'll see yawl later."

Gail was wearing her anger like a knight wearing a suit of armor into battle when the three stumbled into her kitchen. "I was worried to death about you," she hissed at Mark.

"I'm fine," Mark stammered. "Don't worry about me."

"You're drunk," her voice rising. "You're all drunk." Larry was helping himself to the spread she had placed on the table and Joey stood in front of the open refrigerator looking for something. "What has gotten in to you all?"

"What has gotten in to you?" Mark bellowed back at his mother. "Are you mad because we're drunk or because we didn't ask you first?"

"How dare you speak to me with that tone of voice."

"Damn Mom," Joey piped in. "You're beginning to act like Laura the way you stay mad all of the time."

The argument ended suddenly when Emily toddled into the room. "Do you want something to eat?" Mark asked her.

"She's already eaten," said Gail lowering her voice.

Joey slammed the door of the refrigerator, "I think I'll just go on home."

"What?" Gail asked. "You haven't eaten anything."

"I know, but Laura's gonna be mad too. Why should I stay here and listen to you when I'm gonna have to go home and hear her?" He knew that Laura would be mad because he had left her with the children for so long.

"You really shouldn't be so hard on Laura," Mark said.

"I can't believe you're takin' up for her," Joey replied.

"I'm not taking up for her, Joey. I'm just saying, you don't know how lucky you are to have someone to go home to. Even if things aren't the best in the world, you still don't have to go home to an empty house. You don't have a clue what it's really like to be alone. Well, let me tell you. It's scary. It's scary as hell and you ought to go home to Laura and talk things out with her. You guys should try to work things out because neither one of you really know what it's like. And, believe me, you don't want to. Besides, your kids need you. They don't need to grow up hearing you guys fight all of the time."

Joey knew Mark was right. He said his good-byes and left. Mark had given him a lot to think about. Sometimes he wished Laura was not so hard to deal with, but he did love her in his own peculiar way. They had just gotten into the habit of arguing instead of communicating. Yea, Mark was right, he thought as he drove home. We do need to work on things.

Sure enough, Laura was angry with Joey when he got home. But, she became infuriated when he told her about Mark burning Lyn's clothes and belongings. "What?" she shrieked. "Is he out of his mind? Emily may want some of those things when she grows up. I might have wanted some of them. What was he thinking?"

"You know damn well what he was thinking. She was a liar and a cheat and he doesn't want to be reminded of it on a daily basis."

"You have such a way with words, Joey. I know Lyn wasn't perfect, but she was my best friend. And I loved her, even if no one else did."

"We all liked Lyn," replied Joey. "What was not to like? And Mark loved her very much, but he's hurting, Laura. He feels betrayed and he has to deal with it the best way he knows how. And besides, Dad and I did retrieve some of the pictures and stuff for Emily. I figure Mark will want them himself in time, but he's got to get over being so mad first. He's got to be able to grieve or he's never going to be able to get on with his life. And right now, he's too mad to grieve."

Laura began to cry. "Don't cry," Joey tried to comfort her. "Dad took several things for Mom to save. Look Laura, we'll get through this. It's just gonna take some time." Joey thought about what Mark had said again. "Why don't you see if you can get a baby-sitter this weekend and we'll go out for dinner? Maybe we'll see a movie if you want. Would that help you to get your mind off of everything?"

Laura looked at him as if he'd lost his mind. "It's been a long time since we've done anything together," she said.

"I know. But maybe it's time we do. We need to start spending more time enjoying life and less time bickering about it, don't you think? With everything that's happened lately, I've really started thinking about just how short life is."

"You're right," said Laura. "We need to start spending more time together with the boys too. You know, as a family. They need both of their parents. Poor Emily only has one. Bobby has really taken this hard too," she explained through the tears. "He's had so many questions. His teacher called me today and said that he wouldn't go out for recess. He wanted to just sit and stare out the window. And when I picked him up, he started asking me what heaven was like and wanted to know if Lyn was missing Zach, Emily, and he as much as they missed her. I wanted to cry."

"Who was that on the phone at this hour?" asked Martha as Sam walked into the bedroom.

"Just some business I needed to take care of," Sam answered pulling off his robe.

"How did you find Mark when you went to see him?"

"Oh, he's gonna be all right. He just needs some time." Sam climbed into bed next to Martha and kissed her goodnight.

"Is the light going to bother you if I read a while?" Martha asked. But Sam was already asleep.

"What on earth were you dreaming about last night?" she asked him over breakfast the next morning.

Sam thought for a minute then reluctantly answered, "I don't remember. Why?"

"You tossed and turned and fought the pillows all night long. You kept mumbling something about somebody never going to get away with it. And you'd see to it."

"I did?" He chuckled. "I don't have any idea what I could

have been talking about."

# Chapter 5

"What's happening to this family?" Gail cried as Martha filled her coffee cup. "Larry is drinking worse again and he's being a bad influence on Joey and Mark. They won't listen to me anymore when I try to talk to them. Mark is not the same person he used to be. He's angry and bitter and he won't even bring Emily to see me anymore. Lyn's death has ripped my family apart."

"Now, now," soothed Martha. "When you've lived as long as I have, you'll see people go through all kinds of different phases. Our family is no different. I know that you're having trouble dealing with your own loss, but try to think of Mark. Men have always been told to hide their emotions. Be strong. Don't cry. The only acceptable way he has of dealing with this is to be angry. That's just the way men are."

"But does he have to direct that anger at me? He's my son. All I want is for him to be happy again. It's just breaking my heart to see him in such pain. When he was small, I could put a Band-Aid on his hurts and make them all better. But now that he's grown, there's nothing I can do for him. I just feel so helpless."

"Don't rush him," replied Martha. "You can't put a time limit on grief. Recovery is a slow, difficult process. Look Gail, no one can ever be prepared to have their life changed like this. It's a shock to the system. And it's going to take Mark a long time to come to grips with it before he can ever live again. He's not the same person he once was. He's got to find out just exactly who he is now. But, I promise. He will figure it out and he will get through this. In the mean time, all you can really do is try to be as patient and supportive as possible."

"I've never known anyone I could talk to like I can talk to you, Martha. You always know exactly what to say to make me feel better."

Martha moved to the other side of the kitchen and came back with a giant slice of chocolate cake for each of them. "And," she said with a smile, "if all else fails, there's always chocolate."

Sam parked his truck and went inside Lakeland's only café. He spoke to everyone he knew then found a seat in a booth facing the door. "Are you by yourself today?" asked Katie as she hurried over to the booth with a cup of coffee for Sam.

"I'm meeting a friend," he told her. Katie was the granddaughter of an old buddy of Sam's. She'd been waitressing at the Lakeland Café for several years and knew all of the regulars, how they took their coffee, and usually what they wanted to eat, even before they ordered it.

"Will there be anything else for you?" she asked Sam knowing already what the answer would be.

"No thank you. Just coffee," Sam replied as he looked up to see who was coming in the door. A large, middle aged man dressed in a cowboy hat and duster stood in the doorway looking around. As soon as he spotted Sam, he nodded, then walked over and took a seat in the booth facing him. "How was the drive over from Lexington?" Sam asked.

The man started to speak, but Sam stopped him. Katie made her appearance with a coffeepot in one hand and a cup with saucer in the other. "Would you like any cream or sugar sir?" she cheerfully asked the stranger.

"Black is fine," was his answer and Katie disappeared behind the counter again. "The trip over was fine."

"I'm sorry for calling you so late last night," Sam began.

"No problem. What did you need to talk to me about?"

"Well, remember that money I loaned you last year to pay off your debt at the track and get back on your feet again?"

"I sure do. I don't know what I would have done without you either. I'm gonna pay you back, too. Every nickel I owe you, Sam. I made a promise. And Davis Reed doesn't go back on his word."

"Slow down. Slow down, son. That's not why I called you."

"It isn't?" a skeptical Davis asked.

"I don't want the money back." Sam paused. "I want a favor instead."

"What kind of favor?"

"It's very simple," explained Sam. "I just need you to pay someone a visit and talk to him a little bit. He needs to be convinced that he doesn't need to be living in Lakeland any longer. Are you game?"

Davis thought a minute. "I don't have to kill him, do I?"

"I doubt that you'll even have to rough him up any."

"And for this, the slate is wiped clean? I won't owe you anything?"

"That's right. We'll be even."

Davis shrugged. "Okay. I can handle that."

The two gentlemen sat quietly as Katie passed through refilling cups. Then they resumed their conversation. The transaction was complete in only a few minutes with exact details to be relayed on strictly a need to know basis. "Don't you worry, Sam," said Davis standing up. "It'll be taken care of." They shook hands and Davis was on his way back to Lexington as though the meeting had never taken place.

Sam knew he'd never get his money back any other way. And he knew that Davis Reed was mean enough to make a believer out of Jason Kelley. He would simply have Davis explain to Mr. Kelley that his behavior was totally unacceptable and that he was no longer welcome in Lakeland. And that it would be to his benefit to leave town and never return.

Sam finished up his coffee and made his way up to the counter stopping to speak to a few old cronies on the way. He paid his bill and walked toward the door of the café. "Come back to see us," Katie yelled behind him. "And tell Mark I said hello."

Maybe Martha was right Gail thought. Maybe I should just try to be more patient and give Mark more time to adjust to this new life. She wandered aimlessly through the big house she and Larry had built almost thirty years ago. It had been so full of joy when the boys were small, and now, as she went from room to room, it seemed as cold and empty as her heart felt. The joy had all turned to sorrow.

I need more to do she mused. Maybe I should take up gardening like Martha did after all of her children left home. I'd never have the green thumb she's got, Gail thought. Then she wondered how Martha seemed to have such an unwavering faith in God. After everything the woman had been through, she still had the strongest convictions of anyone Gail knew. Gail would have liked to be more like Martha, but she could never admit it. To reveal that would mean having to confess her own inadequacies.

She looked down from her bedroom window to see the trees in her backyard where the hammock used to hang. Joey was conceived in that hammock, she remembered. Then, looking over at the pool, she could almost see a two-year-old Mark swimming for the first time. And now she had grandchildren that were learning to swim. Gail turned and walked over to the mirror. Who was that lonely old lady looking back at her? She gasped at the dark circles and bags under her eyes. She was tired, and her feelings of sadness were magnified by the fact that she couldn't sleep. Her yearly checkup would be soon, and she was hoping the doctor would give her something to help her cope.

Mark was in the stables brushing down the horses as Joey brought them in from the exercising arena. Both had hangovers from the night before and neither were saying much. The radio was tuned in to a popular country and western station and Garth Brooks was "working on a full house." Larry backed his truck up to the entranceway and got out. The hired hand rushed to help him unload the new saddles he'd just purchased as part of the grandchildren's Christmas from he and Gail. All three saddles were specially designed and sized for each child. Larry showed the help exactly where to store the saddles in the tack room then telephoned Gail to see if she wanted to come see them.

Mark stared at his father. "What'd you call her for?" his voice clipped.

"I thought she might want to see the new saddles, Mark. After all, she is the one who designed them and had them made. She's gonna have blankets made to go with them too. And they're gonna have the kid's names monogrammed across the back corner."

"That'll be real nice. I just really didn't want to have to deal with her after last night."

"Well, don't worry about it. She's been high strung ever since I've known her and I don't expect she's gonna change now."

"Well she's driving me crazy. She's done nothing but hover over me since Lyn died. Why can't she realize I'm a grown man? Why does she think she has to control my life?"

"Why don't you just do what Joey does? Your mother treats him the same way, but he's learned to ignore it and go ahead and do what he wants to anyway. In fact, I think he's got to where he even lets her get her way on occasion. As long as he's getting what he wants out of the deal."

"Did I hear my name mentioned?" asked Joey leading another horse back into the stables.

"Yea," replied Mark. "Is that the last one?" he asked patting the horse on the rear. "I thought I might get out of here a little early today."

"What's your hurry?" Joey wanted to know.

"No hurry. I've just got some stuff I need to do."

"Go ahead then. I'll finish up here."

"Thanks man." Mark jumped in the truck and pulled out of

the driveway just as Gail was pulling in. He was relieved he had been able to get out of there before she arrived. Mark hated confrontation and especially with his mother. He drove home and went straight to the shower wondering if he should pick up Emily from the daycare or wait a while. He showered and dressed then went to the kitchen to fix himself a sandwich.

Suddenly, Mark was very aware of the silence, the deadly silence he'd become far too familiar with these past few months. It seemed to follow him home every night and resonate off every wall and through every fiber of his being. A God-awful silence. Maddening. Like some kind of beast stalking its prey. It would steal its way into Mark's house and creep into his very soul. He left his sandwich and drove into town for Emily.

# Chapter 6

"Code Blue," screamed the nurse into the loud speaker. Then she grabbed the crash cart and ran down the hall toward Mr. Kelley's room. "The monitor is going crazy," she told the doctor as he hurried to join her. "His heart is racing faster and faster. Oh my God, he just flat lined."

The doctor grabbed a syringe, filled it, and popped it into Jason Kelley's arm. "Let's start CPR, " he cried, while the nurse prepared the paddles. "Clear," he screamed, and he shocked the lifeless body, and immediately a rhythm resumed on the monitor.

Jason Kelley started to breathe again. He took several short gasps of air and opened his eyes. He tossed his head back and forth and tried to get out of bed. "Calm down Mr. Kelley," ordered the nurse. "Calm down."

But he fought desperately to get out of bed as he moaned "He's going to kill me. Help me. That man is here to kill me." His body was weak and he couldn't put up much of a fight.

"Poor man," said the nurse. "He's had so much medication he's delirious."

Mark jumped from his bed when the phone rang and answered it quickly, so it wouldn't wake Emily. Who in the world could be calling at this hour he thought as he looked at the clock showing 11:15? "Mark," a really sweet voice whispered. "Are you alone?"

"Yes," he said clearing his throat. "Who is this?"

"It's Jennifer. Remember? I talked to you about a month ago."

"Oh yea," he said. "I remember you."

Jennifer was a tall, thin, blonde bombshell that had rubbed

all over Mark after the funeral. She was a friend of Lyn's in high school, but had moved to New York after graduation, hoping to begin a modeling career. Now she was back in Lakeland with stories of how the modeling circuit was just not for her, but everyone knew her parents had just gotten her out of jail for prostitution.

"I was just wondering," Jennifer said "if you might like some company?"

"I don't think so," said Mark. "Emily is here and she's a very light sleeper. Anyway, I'm not quite ready for company yet, if you know what I mean."

"No problem," she cooed. But you've got my number, right?"

"Yea. Thanks for calling. Maybe another time," he said and hung up the phone.

He lay there in the bed staring up at the ceiling for what seemed to be hours thinking about everything that had happened. He was lonely. He did need a woman. But what would people think, he wondered. During the last month, rumors had really been circulating about Lyn and Jason Kelley. He'd finally had to tell Laura not to tell him anything else that people said. He simply did not want to hear about it any more.

He figured he was probably free to do anything he wanted to do. Look at what Lyn had done, he thought. People really shouldn't blame me. After all, he thought, I'm a man, and I do have needs. Maybe I will decide to date someone.

Mark tossed and turned, and again his mind went to Jason Kelley and Lyn, and he didn't like what his imagination was doing. Kelley should have to pay for this. And he should pay for Emily growing up without her mother. Some day, when the time is right, I'm gonna make him pay for what he's done.

Damn, I wasn't lonely until she called and woke me up. Mark took a blanket to the den and lay down on the couch. He turned on the TV and watched music videos until he finally fell back to sleep.

It was fall and there was still a lot to be done at the ranch before bad weather set in. Mark and Joey spent a lot of time together talking as they worked on the fences. Mark told Joey about the call from Jennifer and the other women that had called since then. "You probably didn't know there were so many eligible women in Lakeland," Joey joked.

"That's part of the problem," Mark laughed. "Most of them aren't eligible. I may have been out of circulation for a while, but even I know you don't go trespassing on somebody else's property."

"I've got someone you need to meet," Joey said with a smirk. "In fact, I think you may already know her."

"Who is that?"

"It's Laura's sister, Christie. You remember her don't you? She was at Lyn's funeral, but I think you met her when Laura and I got married."

"Yea. I did see her at the funeral and I knew she looked familiar, but I didn't know why."

"She's coming over to our house tonight to do something to Laura's hair," Joey said. "You should drop by later."

Mark stuttered for a minute, then finally said, "I'm not so sure that's a good idea."

"Well, if you don't like her, you don't have to ask her out. She's been married once, but it didn't last very long. And she's got a little girl about the same age as Emily. She's real independent and I don't think she'd want anything long term in a relationship. She might just be someone you could have a good time with, without having all the strings attached."

"I am kind of attracted to her," Mark admitted. "Okay, maybe I will drop by for a minute, but no promises. She's not as dingy as Laura, is she?" he asked with a smile.

"Now that's not a very nice thing to say." Joey grinned real big and said, "No. No she's not."

"I've been thinking about what you said about me and Laura,"

Joey continued. "We've talked. And we're gonna try to work things out. She's got a lot of growing up to do, but I do love her. I mean, hell, she's the mother of my kids. And she is a good mother."

"Hey, I'll support you every way I can, man. I hope it works out for you two. As tough as it may seem sometimes, it's still better than having no one, believe me."

It was almost seven-thirty that evening before Mark and Emily arrived at Joey's house, but he was soon glad he decided to go. Having no doubt that Mark would show up, Joey had thrown an extra steak in the marinade for him. He knew Mark got very tired of eating alone. Even if he and Christie didn't hit it off, Joey knew he'd stay for supper. Since the girls were just about to finished coloring Laura's hair, the guys decided to light the grill and kick back on the deck with a drink while the children played. Even Christie's little girl was having a good time now that Emily had gotten there to play with her.

During supper, Mark discovered that Christie was very easy to talk to. She was witty and charming and he found himself very relaxed around her. Okay, maybe it was the double martini that Joey gave him earlier, but either way, he was having a good time. And as it started to get late, he found himself not wanting the night to end.

"Do you mind if I walk you to your car?" Mark asked Christie when she announced she had to go home.

"That'd be great," she answered. Once outside, Mark could feel Laura's eyes gazing at them. "Is that Laura peeking through the window?" asked Christie.

"I haven't turned around to look, but I would almost count on it." Christie laughed and started to speak, but Mark interrupted. "You know," he said. "It's been a long time since I've been on a date. And I'm really not sure how to say this, but I had a really good time tonight. And I was wondering," he paused nervously, "well, I was just wondering if you might like to do something sometime."

"Sure," said Christie. "I think I'd like that very much. Just give me a call. Laura can give you the number."

"Okay Laura," Mark said as he went into house. "Get your face out of the window and get me Christie's phone number."

"Did you like her?" Laura squealed anxiously.

"Yea," he said. "I'm surprised, but I did."

"Why are you so surprised?" Laura and Joey asked at exactly the same time.

"I don't know. I guess I just wasn't expecting to have such a good time. She's fun to talk to, though. I think I may ask her out sometime. She doesn't seem like she'd want to get too serious. And that's what I need. I don't want anybody to expect anything out of me right now."

"See," Joey gloated. "I told you so."

When Mark left and the children were in bed, Laura opened up to Joey. "I'm glad they liked each other, but it was really kind of weird."

"What do you mean weird?" asked Joey.

"Looking over the table at the two of them instead of looking at Mark and Lyn. I don't know if I can get used to that or not."

"I doubt that it will be anything for you to get used to seeing too often," Joey said. "I think Mark plans to keep this totally casual. And as long as that's what the both of them agree on, then no one should get hurt."

"Christie won't get hurt," Laura replied. "She's still too hung up on her ex-husband to fall in love with anybody else. I don't think she'll ever love anyone but him."

"Delores told me that Eleanor saw you having coffee with some strange man at the café the other day," Martha informed her husband.

"Is that right?" Sam asked. "It's a good thing that I've never been inclined to run around on you Martha. You'd have known about it before I even got home," he said with a smile.

"And we both know, Sam Lake, that you'd never go looking at any other woman when you've got all you could ever handle right here," she giggled.

"I loaned a guy some money back a few years ago," Sam explained to Martha. "He'd gotten in way over his head at the track and was about to lose everything he had. I know I'm never going to see that money again, but you know that you and I don't really need it. We've got everything we want. Trouble is, since my back has slowed me down some; there are just certain things I'm not up to doing like I used to. So, I told him he could work it off. That way he gets what he needs and so do we."

"That's my Sam. Always helping somebody out." She beamed with pride and then as an afterthought, "Oh, that reminds me, Sam. The Lakeland City Council called this afternoon to talk to you about being the Master of Ceremonies for the New Years Eve bash in the park this year."

"Isn't it a little early to be planning New Years Eve?"

"Not really. It's the new millennium and the Council is going all out. They're planning all kinds of activities and I'm sure it's going to take a lot of time to organize everything."

"What did you tell them?"

"I told them you'd call them back. I think it would be wonderful if you would do it. But, I'm not about to answer for you."

"Okay then," he said. "I'll call them back."

# Chapter 7

Mark bundled Emily up in her coat and gathered her favorite dolls to carry to Joey and Laura's. He'd been looking forward to seeing Christie for days, and since Laura had agreed to baby-sit for him, plans had been finalized for dinner and a movie. He was feeling a little ridiculous, like a grown man having to play high school games again. Having already been married, dating didn't seem quite the same. The rules had changed and he wasn't real sure what they were anymore.

Mark was right on time to pick Christie up, but she wasn't ready yet, so he waited in the living room while she finished dressing. "Are you absolutely certain you want to see this movie?" Christie asked as she entered the room.

"We can do something else if you want to," Mark said standing up.

"I thought you might enjoy this more," she said pulling open her coat and dropping it on the floor. Christie was wearing a black lace bustier with matching lace thongs. A garter belt stretched to meet a pair of lace topped stockings. And a pair of black leather pumps completed the ensemble.

"Damn," Mark said. "You thought right. This sounds like a much better idea."

Christie strolled over to the entertainment center and turned on some music. Then she fixed drinks for the two of them. "I'd like to make a toast," she said, handing Mark his drink. "Here's to the beginning of a great friendship."

"I'll drink to that," said Mark raising his glass to meet hers.

"How was the movie?" Laura chirped when Mark picked up Emily.

"What movie?" Then catching himself, "Oh, the movie. It

was good," he said. "It was real good. But, I'm really tired. I think I'll just get Emily and go on home. Thanks again for keeping her."

"Anytime," said Laura following him around. "Did you have a good time?"

"We had a great time. I've got to get to bed, though. I've got a big day ahead of me tomorrow." Mark didn't want to have to answer any more of Laura's questions. But, he couldn't wait to tell Joey all about it.

He put Emily to bed. Then he flipped on the TV, his nightly companion, and made his bed on the couch. There was something about the couch that seemed comforting to him. Maybe it was just the sounds from the TV that made him feel like he wasn't quite so alone. He wasn't exactly sure how to take what had just happened with Christie, but he decided not to overanalyze the situation. If a casual affair is what she wanted, he was certainly game. No point in looking a gift horse in the mouth, he thought. I'll simply enjoy it while it lasts. He closed his eyes and could still see Christie's tanned, muscular body.

He was still asleep the next morning when Joey knocked on the door. "Shh," Mark said as he unlocked the door and motioned Joey to come in. "You're gonna wake Emily up."

"Too late," said Joey looking up to see Emily totter down the hall.

"It's Saturday, man. Is there some reason you're up so damned early?"

"We promised Dad we'd go pick up the new trailer this mornin'. They've got her ready and I can't wait to see it. Dad said it's a real Cadillac."

"Damn, I forgot," Mark said. "It'll just take me a minute to grab a shower. Why don't you put on a pot of coffee and I'll be right back."

"Did you have a good time last night?" Joey yelled down the hall. "Laura said you wouldn't say much."

Mark stuck his head back around the corner. "I had a helluva good time last night. She is hot."

"I told you so," said Joey.

Jason Kelley waited until visiting hours were over and everyone except employees were gone from the hospital. After weeks of being in and out of the hospital, Kelley's heart rate had finally returned to normal and he'd been unhooked from all the monitors and machines. Now in a private room, Kelley had only one IV remaining.

He carefully removed the needle from his arm then ripped off the tape pulling hair and skin with it. Then he cautiously got out of bed and quietly retrieved his clothes from the closet. He tiptoed to the door and slowly opened it just enough to peek out. He saw no one, so he opened the door wide enough to walk through and look up and down the hall. No one stirred. Then, he took a deep breath and quietly walked to the end of the hall. He turned to look toward the nurse's station. No one had seen him. He quickly ducked into the stairwell, stopping only long enough to grab the door as it threatened to double-cross him by slamming shut. He eased the door closed and started his grueling descent down five flights of stairs.

Kelley's body was weak and he had to move slowly. His heart was beating in his throat and this scared him. He could imagine himself lying on the stairs and having another heart attack, but still, he kept moving until he reached the first floor. No one knows me here, he thought. It will be easy to walk straight through the lobby and right on out the front door. And that's precisely what he did. Kelley then hailed a cab and climbed into the back seat. "The Marriott," he breathlessly told the cabby.

"Adriane," Kelley said into the phone as soon as he got into his hotel room. "I've left the hospital."

"Jason, is that you?" she spoke with sleepy uncertainty. "What's going on?"

"Listen to me Adriane. I'm at the Marriott in Lexington. I need you to bring me some clothes first thing in the morning."

"What are you talking about Jason? What have you done now?"

"I don't want to get in to it over the phone," said Kelley. "Just be here in the morning with me enough clothes for a couple of weeks. Be sure to bring me some shampoo and stuff. Just bring everything I'll need for a couple of weeks traveling."

"Are you out of your mind?"

"Look," he said, getting irritated with her. "Be here. I'm in room 204. I'll explain everything in the morning. Bring the boys with you. I have to be gone for a little while and I want to see them before I leave. And Adriane, don't tell anyone about this. Do you understand me? No one."

Kelley laid across the bed and tried to sleep. But his thoughts returned to the last time that he'd talked to Lyn. And as he closed his eyes, he vividly remembered those crashing sounds at the moment her phone went dead. "Oh God," he said out loud. "How am I ever going to get those sounds out of my head?"

Then, there was a knock at the door. Kelley walked to the door and looked through the peephole. No one was there. He opened the door just enough to stick his head out and look around. Still he saw no one. All of a sudden, a man appeared out of nowhere. He was dressed in black and a ski mask covered his face.

The powerful man kicked his door wide open and shoved a powerless Kelley back into his room. He threw Kelley onto the bed and quickly closed the door behind him. Kelley slid his frail body backward across the bed and grabbed for the telephone. But the intruder snatched the cord out of the wall. Struggling to get out of this madman's reach, Kelley rolled off the bed, grabbing the lamp off the nightstand, and landing on the floor. Kelley swung the base of the lamp upward, but the masked man caught the lamp and threw it against the wall. Too frightened to scream, Kelley stared his rival in the eyes as the man's hands closed around his throat.

Kelley struggled to get up. He was coughing and gasping

for air and his heart was beating faster than ever before. Oh how horrible, he thought, as he wiped the sweat from his forehead then lay back down. What a terrible nightmare. He fixed his eyes on the ceiling above him and was contemplating his subconscious battle when a peck on the window startled him back to reality again. It's raining he thought. It's just raining.

The next knock at the door came a few minutes after eight the next morning. "Who is it?" Kelley yelled at the door.

"It's me, Adriane," came the answer from the other side.

Kelley opened the door for Adriane and the boys. He hugged his boys and kissed Adriane on the cheek. "I'm going to take a shower while you order breakfast for everyone," he told her. "Then we'll take the kids down to the playground and let them play while we talk."

Once at the playground with his boys, and out of hearing range, Kelley told a skeptical Adriane about the warning from his late night visitor in the hospital. "Why would anyone want to run you out of town?" she asked.

"The Lake family is blaming me for Lyn's death," he told her. "I don't know why they think I had anything to do with it."

"I think there's something here you're not telling me," said Adriane.

"I've told you everything you need to know," Kelley snapped. "Now, this is my plan."

Kelley explained to Adriane that he would call the law firm and tell them that he was out of the hospital, but that he still needed a couple of months to recuperate. And after thinking about it all night, he'd decided to make some calls to several headhunters he knew. They would be able to get back in touch with him by calling his cell phone no matter where he was, and he was not yet sure where that would be.

Adriane demanded to know more than Kelley was sharing. "What are the children and I to do, Jason? Just wait until we hear from you? What if something happened to me or one of the boys?"

"I'll call home as often as I can and you'll always be able to reach me by phone. I'll get settled in somewhere as soon as possible and I'll be back for you. There's plenty of money in your account. You shouldn't have to worry about a thing."

"I don't want to be moving the children during the holidays," Adriane whined.

"I don't either," said Kelley. "But it's best that I get out of town for a while."

"Did you kill her?"

"No, I didn't kill her."

"Were you screwing around with her? You might as well tell me the truth because I can tell when you're lying."

Kelley wasn't going to admit to a thing. "The bottom line is this. The Lakes are very well thought of. And if they want me out of town, then I have no choice but to leave. It's no telling what those people are capable of."

"Well, what the hell did you expect?"

Adriane left the playground that day, not knowing when she would see her husband again. But she insisted that he be the one to tell the children he'd be gone for a while. She had gotten used to fending for herself over the years, but she knew the boys would miss their father. It wasn't fair for them, she thought. They needed the chance to develop friendships and put down roots instead of moving constantly. She'd worked hard to make their house a home and now Jason was taking it away from them.

Kelley called the law firm from the hotel and used the rest of the day to contact old acquaintances, just to see where he stood, as far as relocating. One of the headhunters he talked with had done business with John Forbeson, a guy Kelley went to law school with. John moved to Key West, Florida after school to start his own firm. "The winters are cold and nasty in Kentucky," he told the headhunter. If this doesn't work out, he thought, it will be a great vacation while I wait for this Lyn mess to blow over. At 9:32 PM, Kelley boarded a plane and headed south.

# Chapter 8

"What do you mean you can't find anything physically wrong with me?" Gail asked Dr. James as she sat down in his office.

"Gail," he said hesitantly. "I've asked you to step into my office to talk to you because I know you've been under a lot of stress since the death of your daughter-in-law."

"It's been almost three months since Lyn died," she blurted fighting back the tears. "Now, am I menopausal or not?"

"Tests show that you are in the early phases of menopause. However, the hormone replacement you've been taking is keeping your estrogen levels where they need to be. We've run every test in the book and frankly, I can't find any physical problems. But, from the things you've told me, Gail, and judging from your weight loss and insomnia, I think you may be suffering from depression. I can start you out on some medication to help relieve some of your symptoms, but I strongly suggest you let me make an appointment for you with an associate of mine. He's a psychiatrist and he specializes in grief counseling."

Gail sat there with her mouth open not saying a word. Was he implying she was crazy? Who the hell did he think he was? "You've had a lot of changes in your life recently," said Dr. James. "Although no one really understands depression completely, it's believed that certain environmental stresses such as the loss of a loved one can cause or at least contribute to depression."

"Do you think I'm crazy?"

"I said the problem isn't physical," Dr. James answered. "But it's a very real medical disorder that you can not control. And if not treated properly, it could become severe. This is nothing to be ashamed of, Gail," Dr. James said trying to console her. "There are some physical conditions, which can aggravate depression, such as an unhealthy thyroid, mononucleosis, and hepatitis to name a few. But, all of your tests are well within their normal limits. Therefore, I can only suspect that your depression has been caused from the stress you've been under recently. Still, I would be much more comfortable if you saw someone other than myself for a final diagnosis. Would you like for me to make you an appointment or do you know someone else you'd rather see?"

"Your associate will be fine," Gail muttered staring straight ahead. "I'm willing to do whatever it takes to feel good again."

Dr. James left the office for a few minutes, then returned with a name and address written on an appointment card, along with the date and time she had been scheduled. "Dr. Miller can see you next week," he announced, handing her the card. "In the mean time I want you to fill this prescription and take it only as directed."

Gail left Dr. James' office feeling like she had been slapped. She wasn't really shocked at the doctor's assessment, but she felt strangely ashamed of it. She decided not to tell Larry about it until Dr. Miller completed his evaluation. After all, he might have a different opinion all together. But, she did go ahead and fill her prescription.

The next week seemed to drag by and Gail found herself actually looking forward to seeing Dr. Miller. When the day of her appointment finally arrived, she told Larry she was meeting friends for a shopping trip and that she'd be gone for most of the day. Then she left for Dr. Miller's office.

"Dr. James tells me you've had a lot of changes in your life recently, Gail. May I call you Gail?" Dr. Miller asked.

"Yes, that's fine," she replied. "He thinks I'm depressed."

"What do you think about that?"

"I hate to admit it, but I think he may be right."

"Why would you hate to admit that?"

"Because," she paused. "It sounds like I'm not really sick. It sounds like I'm just feeling sorry for myself."

"Have you started taking the antidepressants Dr. James prescribed for you?"

"Yes. And I've been sleeping better these past few nights."

"Good," said Dr. Miller. "Now, why don't you tell me exactly what it is that bothers you the most about your life, Gail."

Reluctantly, she started talking. The more she divulged about herself, the less apprehensive she became. She felt as though Dr. Miller really understood her. The hour seemed to fly, and by the end of her session, she was actually becoming comfortable with him.

"Shall I have my secretary make another appointment for you?" Dr. Miller asked.

"If you think I need one," said Gail.

"Why don't we try a one-hour session every two weeks for now. Keep taking your antidepressants and call me if you should need anything before our next meeting. I think you're going to be fine, Gail. I think you just need a little time."

Mark whistled and danced around as he got out of the shower. He was looking forward to seeing Christie again. "Yep, some days are just better than others," he said out loud to the reflection in the mirror. He'd had a good day and was looking forward to an even better night. The work at the ranch was hard and sometimes the hours long, but all things considered, he was glad he'd decided to stay.

He finished dressing, then gathered up Emily, along with all of her favorite toys and drove to his parents. He found his mother in the kitchen. "You look nice," Gail said upon his arrival. "Is that a new shirt you're wearing?"

"Laura bought it for Joey, but he didn't like it," Mark answered.

"Where are you going tonight?"

"We're going to a party down by the lake."

"Whose party?"

"God mother," he yelled. "It's at some friends of Christie's. Stop interrogating me."

"Well when do you plan to pick Emily up?"

"I tell you what," Mark said angrily. "Why don't I just take

Emily and go home."

"Why?" Gail defended her curiosities, "If I'm going to be responsible for your child, then I at least need to know where you're going to be and when you plan on coming home."

"Okay," said Mark. "Maybe you do need to know some things. But mother, I'm a grown man. You don't need to know everywhere I go and everything I do."

"What are ya'wl fighting about?" Larry asked coming into the room.

"I'm tired of her having to know every little move I make," Mark said.

"Now you wait just a minute," Gail protested.

"No, mother. I'm serious. I'd rather stay at home and do nothing than to have to put up with you every time I want you to baby-sit. It's just not worth it."

"Just go on, son," Larry intervened. "I'll take care of things on this end." Mark stared at his mother. "I mean it," Larry said. "Get out of here. And have a good time."

Mark left, and Larry mixed himself a drink. "Aren't you going to ask me if I want one?" asked Gail.

"Not with you popping pills like they're candies. Are you going to tell me what's going on, or do I have to keep guessing?"

"It's just something the doctor thought would help me get through this depression I've had. There. I've said it. He thinks I'm sick in the head. Are you happy, Larry? Are you?" she badgered. "Are you happy that you're married to a sicko?" Gail ranted about what the psychiatrist had told her. Then she raved about no one caring about her feelings. When all of her frustrations were vented, she broke down and cried.

"You shouldn't act like that in front of Emily," Larry said calmly. Then he picked up his granddaughter and took her into the den.

# Chapter 9

"I'm planning to prepare a big Thanksgiving meal this year," Martha told Gail over coffee.

"Is everyone going to be able to come?" asked Gail.

"Yes, I think so and it's always so much fun for me to get to fix for everyone."

"It's not going to be fun this year," replied Gail. "I dread it. In fact, I dread all of the holidays. I just don't know how Mark is going to make it through them."

"Are you sure you don't mean that you don't know how you're going to make it through them?"

"How dare you," Gail exclaimed! "You have no idea what it's like."

"I do know what it's like, Gail. And it's all right for you to feel this way."

"I just want to be left alone."

"Gail, after my mother died, I wanted to go dig myself a grave right beside hers and climb into it. It was all I could do just to get up in the morning. I didn't want to see anyone or be a part of anything. I just wanted to be left alone. I thought I would never get over losing her. But eventually, the pain eases. It takes a lot of time and effort, but it will get better. I'll never stop missing my mother, and you'll never stop missing Lyn, but you'll move through the grief and make it to the other side of this horrible storm."

"That's what the doctor keeps telling me," Gail said.

"What?"

"I'm seeing a psychiatrist. And don't look so surprised. I had to talk to someone."

"Well, is it helping?"

"A little. He's given me some pills too."

"What kind of pills?"

"Antidepressants. I know you probably don't approve, Martha, but they're helping."

"Good. I'm glad you're getting some help. I do hope that you will be careful with them."

"You don't have to say it like that," Gail said, knowing exactly what Martha meant by that last comment.

"Don't be so defensive," Martha argued. "I just don't want you to depend on pills to make you happy. If these pills help you to get through this, then by all means, take them. But, don't look inside a bottle of pills to find happiness. Believe me, you're not going to find happiness in a pill, anymore than Larry is going to find happiness in the bottle he keeps hidden under his truck seat."

"I've got to go," Gail said out of the blue. She wasn't mad at Martha. It just irritated her to no end that Martha had implied she might actually allow herself to become addicted to drugs. "What should I bring for Thanksgiving?" she asked on her way to the door.

"Why don't you bring a desert," Martha suggested. "Your deserts are always so good."

God, I'm still so tired, Gail thought when she got home. At first, the antidepressants seemed to help her sleep, but now she remembered waking up at all hours during the night. She ambled into the kitchen and stood looking in the refrigerator, trying to decide what to fix Larry for dinner. It wasn't easy to cook for him now that she had no appetite, but this too she considered a plus. Maybe she could finally lose those few pounds she had gained.

Looking at the clock, she realized it was much too early to start dinner. I know how to pass this time, she thought. I'll start writing the journal that Dr. Miller wanted me to keep. She retrieved the empty journal and sat down at the kitchen table to write her first entry. She stared out the window and tried to analyze her feelings. Then she remembered what the doctor said to do, and she started to write her thoughts as they came to her.

*Today has been a really hard day. That calloused feeling that I have many days, as a means of self-preservation, has eluded me and I want to drink. I want to drink so that I go numb and I don't have to feel anything. I hurt so bad that it's now a physical pain, like a knife that's being jabbed into my heart and slowly moved up and down and around so it would be as agonizing as possible. Then, the knife gets yanked out of my heart and jabbed back in again. Over and Over, again and again, the knife goes in and out, and no matter what I do to stop it, it goes on and on until I think I am going to explode. And then, I break down and cry. And once again I'm calloused.*

"I'll have a margarita," Kelley told the waitress as he kicked back on the porch of a beachfront bar. This is the life, he thought. No wonder so many artists and writers find inspiration here. The weather is perfect, the beaches are great, and nobody can party like the people on Duval Street. This was exactly the type of relaxed atmosphere Kelley had been looking for.

Kelley rented a chalet on the beach, one that had a great view of the topless bathers. And for fun, he was also trying his hand at golf, tennis, and deep-sea fishing for the first time. So it was no wonder that Adriane was tired of being put off every time she mentioned flying to the Keys for a visit. Kelley was enjoying his new life, but he needed to take care of business so he phoned John Forbeson and agreed to meet him for a drink.

"I see you've been working on your tan," John said as he approached Kelley with hand extended. Kelley stood and the two gentlemen shook hands. "This is my partner, Rob Gray," John announced.

"Pleased to meet you Rob," Kelley said. "I hope you gentlemen don't mind that I started without you," he added as his margarita was delivered.

"Not at all," they replied. Then each ordered a beer.

"Jason, I would have known you anywhere," John said as he sat down. "You haven't changed a bit since college."

"You haven't either," said Kelley. "Except for the T-shirt and shorts. It must be great getting to practice law in your flip-flops," he laughed.

"Yes it is. The only time I put on a suit is when I have to make an appearance in the courtroom, and I love it. No one in the Keys expects you to dress any differently. It's a world away from Boston."

Then getting down to business, Kelley asked, "Have you had much time to think about what we discussed on the phone, John?"

"Actually, I have. And I think I may have an opportunity you would be interested in." Kelley listened as John explained the type of help his firm was looking for. Most of his practice would not be those hard core cases that Kelley was used to dealing with. This firm was more laid back. They settled a lot of divorce disputes, estate settlements, and the occasional drunken tourist. John made it very clear that he was not cut out for the stress that's associated with criminal justice. He left that up to the other attorneys on the island. So, if Kelley was more interested in that kind of excitement, then this job was not for him. But, if he liked the idea of a stress free work place, then John would love to have Kelley come on board.

"How many partners are in this firm, other that you and Rob?" Kelley asked.

"Oh," said John. "Rob is not my law partner. He's my life's partner."

"Well, I guess you've changed a little since college," Kelley chuckled. "I apologize."

"No apology necessary," John assured him. "Actually, that's why I chose to move to Key West and start my own practice."

"So," Kelley inquired, "there's no one else in the firm but you?"

"That's right. Well, that is, you and me, if you decide to join me," John joked at Kelley, sensing he'd become ill at ease. "Don't worry," he laughed. "I know you like women."

"As a matter of fact, I'm married to one," Kelley said. "And I have two sons."

"I know that you need time to think about this," John interrupted. "Key West is not for everyone. Take some time, talk it over with you wife, and if you decide you'd like to give it a try, let me know. Then we can discuss salary and benefits."

"Is your wife in town with you?" Rob wanted to know.

"No, she's back in Kentucky with the children."

"Kentucky?" asked John. "The last I heard, you were in Raleigh."

"Long story," said Kelley.

"Well, since you're alone," John said, "would you like to join Rob and I for dinner and drinks tonight?"

"We would love to have you," persuaded Rob.

Kelley thought a minute. "Don't worry," John said. "I promise not to take you to an all gay bar."

"In that case," said Kelley. "Why the hell not?"

# Chapter 10

The tension was so thick in Martha's kitchen you could have cut it with the knife she used to carve the turkey. She moved quickly from one counter to the next, busying herself with Phillip's favorite casserole and the fruit salad that Elizabeth loved. Everyone had his or her preferred dish, and at Thanksgiving, Martha made sure that no one was disappointed. She loved it when her children came home and she loved preparing a special feast, but this year things were different. Someone was missing.

"Mark seems more like his old self lately," Martha shared with Elizabeth when she came into the kitchen.

"How's everyone else been doing?" Elizabeth asked.

"I'm kind of holding my breath on that one," said Martha.

"What do you mean, Mom?"

"I'm afraid Gail is coming apart at the seams. She's been seeing a psychiatrist and he has her on antidepressants."

"What kind of antidepressants?"

"I don't know what kind they are. But I know that since she's been taking them, she's been nervous and mad at the world."

"Oh mother," said Elizabeth. "Gail has always had a chip on her shoulder."

"I know, but it's different this time. It's like she doesn't even care what Mark is going through. She can't get her mind off of herself long enough to care about anyone else anymore. Larry told your father the other day that he and Mark and Joey tried to avoid her as much as possible. Every time they're around her, she tries to pick a fight with one of them. It's almost as if it's the only way she can get enough attention."

"Well, we'd better change the subject," said Elizabeth. "She's coming in the front door."

"Hey everyone," Gail said as she entered the den where all

of the men were gathered in front of the television. She moved through the crowd and joined Martha and Elizabeth in the kitchen. The other daughters-in-law followed shortly with each one asking; "What can I do to help?" Martha assigned each one a chore, and soon the table was set and the meal ready to serve.

The entire family met in the dining room where Sam, Jr. returned thanks to the Lord and asked his blessings on the food. "Everybody dive in," said Sam. "Just don't get in my way." They filled the children's plates and seated the kids in the den. But Sam, as always, sat at the head of the table, and the rest of the brood scattered about the dining room and den. Everyone ate to the point of misery, and Martha was most proud.

Now the men settled back in front of the television for the afternoon football games and the children ran outside to play. This, of course, left the women with clean up detail, giving them a chance to catch up on the latest gossip. Things seemed to be going as smoothly as possible under the circumstances until Martha announced she was making a fresh pot of coffee if anyone cared for any.

"No thanks," said Gail. "But I would like a drink. Would anyone like to join me?"

"Are you sure you need to be drinking right now?" asked Elizabeth.

"Why not? It's Thanksgiving. Let's celebrate."

"But, do you think it's a good idea to mix alcohol with what you're taking?"

"It's just one drink," Gail scoffed. "Besides it's really none of your business."

Elizabeth wouldn't give up. "I'm just concerned about you," she said. "I don't want you to do anything that might harm your health."

"One drink is not going hurt a thing." And Gail left the room to mix herself a drink.

"You need to keep your opinions to yourself," Martha said to Elizabeth.

"Mother," she replied. "What is she on and how much of it is she taking?"

"I tried to talk to her about it one day, but the subject was forbidden. Since then, I've just minded my own business." Laura sat with the other women not saying a word while Martha and Elizabeth hashed over Gail's habits.

"Does Larry know?" Elizabeth asked. "I can't believe he would allow her to mix pills and alcohol."

"He knows," Laura said barely above a whisper. "But he can't do anything about it."

"Don't you all understand what she's doing to herself?" Elizabeth kept on as Gail walked back into the room.

"You're making way too much out of this," Gail said.

"Maybe no one else is making enough out of it. Good grief. People can get addicted to nose spray if they're not careful."

At that, Gail slammed her glass down on the table and hissed, "I'm not a drug addict. How dare you even suggest such a thing! You need to just go back to your perfect little life in your perfect little world and not concern yourself with mine."

Martha, determined to change the subject, started clearing the table and asking how everyone's Christmas shopping was coming along. "I'm almost finished with mine," she announced with pride.

"I haven't even started," said Laura.

"You don't have much longer," Martha said. "Christmas is just right around the corner."

"It's no fun without Lyn. We used to do all of our shopping togcthcr."

"I know it's hard for you," said Martha. "Listen, I know it won't be the same, but would you like to go with me sometime?" Then as an afterthought, "I know. Why don't we all go tomorrow? The after Thanksgiving sales will be starting in the morning and if we all go together, it won't seem like such a chore. We can make a day of it and I'll treat everyone to lunch. Won't that be fun?"

"Yes mother," Elizabeth said. "It does sound like fun. You can count me in."

"Sounds great," everyone else chimed in. "I'm ready for a day out with the girls," said Patty, Michael's wife. "I'll just inform Michael he's going to have to keep an eye on the kids while I finish up some shopping. He can watch them and visit with his dad and brothers while we enjoy ourselves. It'll be good for him."

"It'll be good for Joey too," said Laura. "He doesn't understand how exhausting Bobby and Zach are."

"Then it's all set," said Martha. "Now, if you don't mind Gail, I've got to have another piece of your caramel cake with my coffee. I just love this frosting," she said cutting a giant sized slice. "What the heck. I can diet next week."

Since Sam had quit smoking, Martha refused to let anyone smoke in the house so Elizabeth poured herself a cup of coffee and walked outside to light a cigarette. She shivered from the cold and huddled against a tree to try to block the wind. "You would think as cold as it is, we could stop this nasty habit," Mark said lighting up to join her.

"I didn't even hear you come out," said Elizabeth. "My teeth must have been chattering too loud. How are you doing, bud?"

"I'm all right. Most of the time anyway."

"You want to talk about it?"

"Not really. There's not much to say. Except," he paused, " you know what I think?"

"What's that?"

"I think that people like Mom and Dad don't realize how lucky they are."

"What do you mean?"

"They married the right person the first time and they've been together ever since. I mean, I know it probably hasn't always been easy. I know every marriage has its problems. But, they don't really know what it's like to be alone. They don't really know what being lonely is."

"You're right. They're very fortunate."

Then Mark asked, "You know what its like, don't you Elizabeth?"

"Yea, bud. I guess I do. And I suppose I did like you for a while and tried to analyze it and understand it. Now I've learned to just accept it and enjoy life for what it is. But there's one thing for sure, this hell you're going through now will make you stronger in the long run. It'll make you a better person."

"Well I wish it would hurry up and be the long run," Mark said with a smile.

"I know. It's not going to happen over night, though. They're not called growing pains for nothing."

Mark laughed. "I know. Let's go in; I'm freezing."

On the other side of town, Adriane set the table for a late lunch. She let the children help mash the potatoes and fill the drinking glasses. Jason had promised to call every day, but it had been almost a week since she'd last heard from him. She had called him several times, but he'd not returned any of her messages. She told the boys that she knew he would call them and wish them a Happy Thanksgiving just as soon as he was able.

Adriane knew the boys suspected problems, but still, she made excuses for Jason. Both boys said grace, starting with the oldest, and then Adriane made a game out of naming things to be thankful for. She smiled and played with the boys, as if she was the happiest woman on earth. All the while, her loneliness and resentment toward Jason grew.

I wonder if this is the way Mark Lake feels, she thought. There's a person who must know what loneliness feels like. I wonder what kind of Thanksgiving he is having. That's not all she wondered. She also wondered how deeply her husband had been involved in Lyn's death. She knew there was more to the story than Jason was telling her. But she also knew that the odds of him confessing were about a million to none.

"These islanders really know how to throw a party," Kelley slurred at his newfound friends. John and Rob were used to the spicy cuisine and the rum punch cocktails, but Jason Kelley was just beginning to find out what Key West was all about. Unlike the traditional Thanksgiving feast his family was sharing back in Lakeland, he was gorging himself on the freshest of seafood. He couldn't get enough of the lush tropical flavors and the conch fritters. Those were his favorites. He could eat them by the bucket full. Each restaurant or pub in the Keys was known for its specialty, and from the fresh baked breads to the richest roasted coffees and organic herbal teas, the island had everything imaginable. Jason Kelley planned to try it all.

"You haven't bar hopped," said John, "until you've bar hopped in Key West."

"There's no place like it," Rob chimed in.

"I still have to save room for crayfish and beer," said Kelley. "Let's go down to that place on the waterfront where clothing is optional. I want to enjoy the scenery while I eat."

The waterfront pub was a favorite hangout. Locals went there, and there was always something going on, like a "Best Body" contest that was held at least once a week. Local bartenders also gathered there to compare new drink recipes, and patrons were delighted because they got to drink all the free samples they could hold. The waterfront catered to the most diverse crowd in town, even the 'straights' went there, so Kelley would be comfortable.

"The waterfront it is," said Rob. "But, you'd better slow down on your drinking or you're not going to be able to enjoy the "Battle of the Bands"."

"Oh, you've got to see that," John said. "They've held this contest here every winter, but this year they decided to make it part of the island's Thanksgiving celebration. It's a blast."

"I'll be fine," Kelley said. "I've got enough food in me to soak up all the alcohol. Besides, I wouldn't want to miss any part of this Thanksgiving. Oh man," he said. "I forgot to call Adriane and the boys. Oh well; I'll just do it in the morning."

It was 5 am when a drunken Kelley made it back to his chalet, and with him was a pretty Canadian girl that he'd met and partied with at the pub. When he opened the door, his cell phone, which he'd left for the evening on his night stand, was ringing. Kelley didn't care. He stripped down to his birthday suit and threw his clothes over the phone as if it wasn't there. He fell onto the bed, pulling the girl on top of him, and promptly passed out.

# Chapter 11

"I really had a great time, Mom," Elizabeth said as she packed up her car. "Mom," she continued, "I've got a friend in Louisville that counsels people who've been diagnosed with depression. She deals a lot with anxiety disorders and the like. If you think Gail might talk to her, I'd be glad to give her a call."

"I don't know," said Martha. "It's something to think about. But, I don't think Gail is ready to admit that the pills are not getting to be bottom of the problem. She doesn't realize that they're just covering up her problems temporarily."

"They have their place I'm sure," said Elizabeth. "But, I'm afraid if she doesn't get control of herself, her pills will become the problem."

"I know," said Martha. "I just don't know if we should interfere or not. I've told her how concerned I am, but she just keeps assuring me that I'm making too much out of it."

"Well, just think about it," said Elizabeth. "You'll do the right thing. You always do. I love you," she said climbing into the car. "I'll call you when I get home."

"What are you doing?" Larry asked Gail as he walked by the office.

"Come here a minute," Gail said behind him. Larry turned around and went back into the office. "I'm trying to take care of some end-of-the-year paperwork so I won't have so much to do after Christmas," she explained. "But, things are not adding up as I expected. Have you been giving Mark money other than his paycheck?"

"I've given him a few hundred dollars here and there," Larry admitted. "He's needed a little extra."

"What about Joey? You shouldn't do something for one son

that you don't do for the other one."

Larry grew defensive. "I've helped Joey out when he's needed it."

"Then let me put it this way. You shouldn't be giving Mark money to throw away on booze and women. Your few hundred dollars here and there has added up to several thousand, and now I can't get this damned spreadsheet to balance."

"Just calm down," Larry told her. "I'll help you and we'll get it all straightened out."

"I don't have any more time to fool with it today," she said. "But, promise me we'll sit down next week and try to fix this mess."

"I can do it right now if you want to," Larry said.

"No. Laura is coming to get me in a few minutes and we're going to the cemetery."

"Okay. Just let me know when you want to do it."

"Has Mark been to the cemetery yet?"

"No. And, he probably won't be going any time soon."

"I bet he hasn't even seen the beautiful tombstone Laura and I picked out."

"He doesn't want to go right now," Larry said. "And you don't need to try to force him. He has his reasons."

"Well," Gail interrupted "he will have to go eventually. One of these days Emily will be old enough to want to see where her mother is buried. And Mark needs to be the one to take her."

Their discussion was cut short when Laura arrived. "Are you ready?" she asked Gail.

"We just need to load these poinsettias," Gail said.

"I'll get them for you." Larry picked up a potted plant with each hand. "You just get the door for me."

"They're beautiful," Laura sang out. "Lyn would have loved them."

"I decided to get red ones," Gail explained. "They look more Christmassy than the pink and white ones." The ladies loaded up and were on their way to decorate Lyn's grave for Christmas.

Gail sobbed at the graveside as she knelt to place the poinsettias, one on each side of the granite rock that declared Lyn's beginning and end of life on this earth. "She was depressed a lot, wasn't she?" Gail asked Laura. Then answering herself, "She didn't know any other way to be. I feel guilty for that, Laura. She needed help and I didn't realize it until it was too late. If only I had recognized her cries for help. Maybe she would still be alive today. Maybe she wouldn't have been in the car that day."

"I feel guilty too," Laura confessed.

"Why do you feel guilty?"

Laura stood silently for a moment looking down at Gail then she knelt beside her and started to cry. "You know all those rumors you heard about Lyn after she died?" she asked. "They were true. She was seeing Jason Kelley. I knew it and I didn't tell Mark."

"What do you mean, you knew?"

"She told me all about it. I even kept Emily for her when she would go to meet him," Laura blurted. "I've wanted to tell you, but I was scared. I didn't know what to do."

"I can't believe you covered for her. I can't believe you've kept this a secret all of this time."

"What good would it have done to tell him? I didn't want to hurt Mark any more than he already was. My God! Hasn't he been through enough?"

"Yes he has. And for that reason, we can never tell him. Telling him now wouldn't do any good. We can never repeat this to anyone. It'll be our secret, Laura."

"No wonder you've felt so guilty," Gail said as she stood and brushed herself off. "Is there anything else you're not telling me?"

"No," said Laura. "I'm sorry, Gail. I'm so sorry! I feel so ashamed."

"Oh stop it," Gail snapped. "You didn't put a gun to Lyn's head and force her to do what she did. She's not the first person to ever be unfaithful. Lyn was always doing just what made Lyn happy. She never really considered what it might do to someone else. And considering the way she was raised, she's lucky she turned out as good as she did."

"I just don't understand how things can get so screwed up," Laura cried. "I want everything to go back to way it used to be when she and Mark first got married. We had so much fun together. I just don't understand what happened."

"Life happened," Gail replied as she turned and started to walk toward the car. "Things changed that awful day Lyn was killed. We all changed. And none of us will ever be the same again."

"Where the hell have you been?" Adriane asked Jason as soon as she realized it was him on the phone.

"I'm sorry I didn't call you on Thanksgiving," Jason said apologetically. "All of the towers were busy because there was so much holiday usage and I couldn't get through."

"You promised you would call home everyday. You're down there having a party while I've been stuck here for weeks."

"Don't be mad, Adriane. I've got some great news. How would you like to live in Key West?"

"Your children are about to forget what you look like."

"Did you hear me, Adriane?"

"Yes, I heard. When are you coming home?"

"In a few days. Now answer my question."

"Have you found a job yet?"

"Yes. But, I told them I'd need to think about it over the holidays and talk it over with you. What do you think?"

"Why don't we talk about it when you get home?"

"Fine. I'll call you back after I make my flight arrangements. Put the boys on for me. I want to tell them all about this place."

# Chapter 12

No place on earth could compare to the inviting ambiance of Martha Lake's home during the Christmas season. The smells of homemade goodies beckoned you to come in. And the warmth that seemed to exude through every room cast a spell on its visitors, making it hard for them to leave. Although the fireplace was no longer needed as a source for heat, Martha insisted on a fire throughout the holidays. It added, in her opinion, that extra touch that gave the living room its cozy glow. And even though most of the upstairs was vacant since the children left home, every room in the house was adorned in the Yuletide spirit.

Every year Sam would ask, "Martha, why do you put all of these decorations everywhere when you know you're just going to have to turn around and take them all down again?"

And every year Martha would answer, "Because Christmas is about family. And every article I've displayed tells a story about our family. Look at this ornament," she would say, holding up a Styrofoam snowman. "Elizabeth made this for me when she was in first grade."

Sam would continue to tease her about her most prized possessions telling her she was just like a kid playing with a toy she hadn't seen for a while. But, when Christmas morning rolled around, there would always be a package under the tree from him containing a new ornament of some sort for her collection.

She got immense enjoyment from this once a year stroll down memory lane. Memories seemed to pour out of each box, as one by one, she carefully opened each individually wrapped item and placed them on just the right mantel or tabletop. Her collection included blown glass figurines that dated back to the time when she was a child, and one highly-treasured brass horse that she and Sam bought on their honeymoon in New Orleans. She loved everything about Christmas as she draped the banister leading upstairs with hand-made garland from the freshest of evergreens. And the garlands had to be fresh each year, because Martha not only wanted her house to have the appearance of Christmas, but she wanted the house to smell like Christmas as well. From her wreaths to rugs, from home made to store bought, Martha tastefully combined the old and the new into a breathtaking collage of holiday splendor.

"The ladies from the Garden Club will be here in about thirty minutes," Martha told Sam, as she bustled about making fresh coffee and putting the finishing touch on her Christmas cake.

"Don't worry," he said in return. "I'll be out of your way."

Martha went into the living room to make one last check before her friends arrived. As she stretched to straighten the angel on top of the tree, her thoughts went back to the first time Lyn visited her home at Christmas time. She remembered as if it were yesterday, the wonder in Lyn's eyes as she had looked about the room in astonishment. I can't believe what it must have been like to grow up in a place like this, Lyn said. Then Martha took her by the hand and led her on a tour of the house, revealing all kinds of interesting stories about the past. Lyn had been much more interested in her family than Laura had been, so Martha shared all sorts of amusing details, which seemed to fascinate the girl.

Martha couldn't help but remember being moved to the point of tears that day by Lyn's comments on her own family history. Lyn remarked that the Lakes were so lucky to have a strong family background. And as Martha reflected on yesteryear, Lyn seemed to hang on every word.

Now, Martha stared at the twinkling lights on her tree with a humbling sadness. How distressing it is that some children do not grow up surrounded by the love and attention they deserve. Then she said a silent prayer of gratitude that, even through the hard times, her family still had each other.

"You've really outdone yourself this year, Martha," replied

the Garden Club members as they oohed and aahed their way through her home. Martha's pleasure rose to pure ecstasy as the ladies complimented her every arrangement.

"I enjoy myself more every year," she confessed, leading the ladies into the dining room. After everyone was seated, Martha served cake and coffee as they discussed what role the Garden Club intended to play in the New Year's Eve "Celebration in the Park".

"I'm trying to tell you the easiest way to balance your books," Larry explained to an already distraught Gail. "The clearer I can make it for you, the easier it'll be."

"Stop talking to me like I'm stupid. It's your fault they're in such a mess anyway." Her frustration quickly escalated to anger. The anger followed by a tear-filled barrage of self-pity.

"You're going to have to straighten up," demanded Larry. "The grieving period is over. When are you going to let go of it and start living again?"

"I didn't know there was a time limit on grief," shouted Gail. "And I can't just let go. My life has changed. All of our lives are changed and I won't just accept it."

"You've got to accept it Gail. You don't have a choice. Do you want to live in this turmoil forever? Do you want your children and your grandchildren to stop coming to see you? That's what's going to happen. No one wants to see you keep putting yourself through this. It must be true what they say about misery loving company, because you're miserable and you're trying to pull everyone else in with you. When are you supposed to go back to the doctor?"

"Next week," Gail snubbed uncontrollably. "He won't give me anymore pills until I go back to see him."

"And that's another thing," Larry said. "If you're going to keep taking those damned pills, then at least take them right."

"What's that supposed to mean?"

"It means, I've kept my mouth shut as long as I'm going to.

It means, stop drinking. You're not supposed to mix those pills with alcohol and you know it. It's almost like you're on some self-destructive mission. You're going to keep on until you can't help yourself. For Christ's sake, Gail. Look at yourself." He snatched her by the shoulders and marched her down the hall to the bathroom. He pointed her toward the mirror and said again, "Look at yourself, Gail."

Gail stared into the mirror, as she had done a few weeks before, and again, wondered who that old lady was looking back at her. "Oh Larry. I feel so responsible."

"For what?"

"For the boys' happiness. I feel responsible for Joey and Mark's happiness. All I ever wanted was for them to be happy. I dedicated my whole life to them, and now they don't need me anymore."

"Listen to me." Larry said shaking her by her shoulders. "You did a great job with the boys. But they're grown men now and they're responsible for their own happiness. You've done all you can do for them. Now is the time we need to be focusing on us and enjoying the fact that they are grown and out of the house. Look, you've never hesitated to tell me when I'm messing up, so I'm going to tell you. Stop worrying so much about where they're going and what they're doing, and start planning a trip for us. We'll take a vacation after Christmas and leave the ranch for them to run. They'll be fine with it. And I'm telling you; it's time we start enjoying life a little bit."

"You're right. Where do we want to go?"

"It's totally up to you," he said. "I'll take you anywhere you want to go. Just pick the place and make the reservations."

Mark had never been jealous of Joey before. But, now he found himself a little envious of the fact that Joey and Laura seemed to be getting along better. He was happy for them, but at the same time, that meant he'd spent less time with his brother. Mark knew he wasn't ready to find anyone to settle down with, but he did long for companionship, especially during the holidays. His fascination with Christie was beginning to fade. Even though his physical desires were being satisfied, he needed someone who could meet his emotional needs as well. It had been fun for a while, but he needed to move on. The time they'd spent together was beginning to leave him depressed, rather than fulfilled, and Mark found himself wondering if he'd ever meet the right woman.

As he sat patiently on the couch waiting for Emily to find her boots, he considered the qualities he would look for in a person the next time he decided to get married. "I'm ready," she announced finally. They were off to find the perfect Christmas tree. Lyn had always used an artificial tree; therefore, Mark wanted a real one. Gail bought some unbreakable ornaments and Emily had been busy in daycare making some of paper. Emily was looking forward to picking out her own tree and having her daddy cut it down for her. And of course, looking very forward to Santa's visit.

As father and daughter set out on their search, they held hands and talked like two adults would, concerning how big the tree should be and where they were going to put it. Emily walked proudly beside her daddy until the weeds and grass were over her head. Mark picked her up and placed her on his shoulders where Emily squealed, "I'm taller than you are, Daddy." He was overwhelmed at how much joy she could find in the simplest of things. Her enthusiasm seemed to wear off on him and he found himself actually enjoying their adventure.

When Emily picked out just the right tree, Mark chopped it down, according to her orders. Then he laughed and said, "Okay. There it is. I chopped it down. Now you have to drag it home."

"Daddy," she said, placing her hands on her hips and giving him a little pout. "It's too big."

"It is? All right, then. I guess I'll have to do it." Mark dragged the tree home and secured it in a holder that Martha had given him. He let Emily pour the water into the holder's reservoir and said, "Now we get to decorate it." Emily jumped up and down, clapping her hands with excitement and she ran to get her handmade stars and clothespin angels.

Mark helped Emily reach the highest limbs as she put on the lights, but Emily was able to hang most of the ornaments herself, which she did with all the care of a professional decorator. Lastly, Mark lifted her upon his shoulders so she could place her angel on the very top of the tree. "This looks like my mommy," she said to Mark. "'Cause she's an angel now."

They plugged in the lights and both stood back to admire their work. "Do you know what time it is?" Mark asked Emily. "It's bath time."

"No," Emily whined. "I want to play a while."

"You have to take your bath so you can go see Santa Claus," Mark told her. "Bobby and Zach will be here in a little bit to get you, and you need to be ready to go."

Joey and Laura arrived at Mark's just as he was drying Emily's hair. Bobby and Zach were bouncing off the walls with excitement. "Are you staying with me?" Mark asked Joey.

"No," Laura answered before Joey had a chance to speak. "I can't handle all three of these kids by myself. Why don't you get ready and go with us?" she asked Mark.

"I thought Mom was going with you," Mark answered.

"She didn't feel well," said Joey. "Why don't you come on and go with us?"

"You guys go ahead to see Santa and I'll get a shower and meet you at the parade."

"Okay," Laura said, grateful for whatever crumbs Mark would throw her. She knew Mark suspected that she knew more about Lyn's business than she would say. And, she knew that he didn't want to be around her. The only reason he did come around was because he loved his brother. Mark wouldn't do anything to hurt Joey and all she could hope for was that one day, they too would be close again. Sometimes she found herself resenting Lyn for leaving her in such an awkward position. And it broke her heart to think that Lyn had just used her, like she did everyone else.

Mark showered and readied himself for the big Christmas parade. He turned off the lights on his tree, then paused for a moment, remembering the Christmas that he'd given Lyn an engagement ring. He was not looking forward to playing Santa Claus this year by himself. At least I won't have to be alone on New Year's Eve, he thought. We will all be at the park celebrating together that night.

The shopping center was crowded and there was a long line of children waiting to see Santa Claus. Laura and Joey were waiting impatiently with the rest of the parents, as one by one, a child climbed upon Santa's lap with special instructions for Christmas. Joey wished he was anywhere else on earth, but these were his children too, so he waited with Laura, fidgeting worse than the youngsters did.

Finally, it was Bobby's turn. He was ready with his list of desires, and of course, he had been a good boy this year. Zach was next and far too terrified to speak when Santa's helper picked him up and sat him on the jolly old elf's lap. In wide-eyed terror, Zack stared at the red-suited man, then jumped from his lap and ran crying back to Laura.

When it came Emily's turn, she happily plopped down on Santa's knee. "And what would you like for Christmas, little girl?" Santa asked.

She spoke very softly and Laura and Joey both leaned toward her so they could hear her Christmas requests and report their findings to Mark. "I would like to have a new mommy," Emily told Santa. "I don't have one anymore and I think that is what I would like to have most of all."

Santa was speechless, not knowing how to respond to the articulate little girl. Joey stared in disbelief at Laura as tears welled up in her eyes. Then she took Emily by the hand and helped her off Santa's lap. "Thank you," Laura said to Santa.

"Don't say it Joey," Laura said.

But he said it anyway. “God. I wasn’t expecting that.”

“I wasn’t either,” Laura whispered as they moved away from the crowd. “If Mark asks, you just tell him she wants more Barbie dolls. She loves them.”

Jason Kelley dreaded the flight home. He dreaded the interrogation he’d receive from Adraine. But most of all, he dreaded keeping a very low profile, because he did not want to be spotted back in Lakeland. He wouldn’t be taking this chance, if it weren’t for his kids. Adriane was right though, he thought. This transition should be made as uncomplicated as possible for their sake.

He finished most of his packing then walked down to the shopping district to get Christmas presents for everyone. He bought a gold conch shell bracelet for Adriane. “When she sees this,” he laughed and told the jeweler, “she’ll forget all about being mad.” The boys were harder to buy for, since he didn’t really know what they were interested in these days.

After much deliberation, he finally decided on a remote controlled airplane for the oldest. Then, remembering that they fought over each other’s gifts every year anyway, he returned to the hobby shop and bought another one just like it. Next on his shopping list were Rob and John. He stopped in the wine shop and arranged for a case of their favorite wine to be delivered to them on Christmas Eve. Last, but certainly not least, he shopped for himself. He loaded up on the finest cigars to be found this side of Havana.

He heaved a sigh of relief when he discovered there was plenty of room in his luggage for the boys’ airplanes. They would be so disappointed if he had to ship them separately and the boys weren’t able to open their presents the minute he got home. Next, he placed Adriane’s bracelet and his cigars in his carry-on.

Soon, Rob and John would be there to take him to the airport, but he still had a few minutes, so he kicked back on his deck for one last ogling at the topless bathers. Kelley hated leaving, he thought to himself. But, I'll be back. Suddenly, he was very much aware of how uncomfortable shoes had become, since he hadn't worn anything on his feet but flip-flops since his arrival in Key West.

When Rob and John arrived, they helped Kelley load his luggage into their minivan. "I really appreciate you guys taking me to the airport," he said as they drove away from the chalet. "I don't mind calling a cab if it's too much trouble."

"It's no trouble at all," they chimed. "We wouldn't want you to leave without us having the chance to say goodbye," said Rob.

"Let's not call this goodbye," John said. "Let's just say we'll see you later."

"Absolutely," Kelley agreed.

Parking was a bit of a problem at the small airport, so Kelley insisted that his friends drop him off at the terminal. "I'll be in touch with you two as soon as Adriane and I have a chance to make arrangements," he shouted and waved back at the minivan as it pulled away. Once inside the airport, Kelley checked his luggage and waited with the rest of the passengers for boarding call.

The small plane was carrying him to a connecting flight in Miami. Kelley was depressed to be leaving the island, but the crowded plane and the rough turbulence was making this trip almost more than he could bear. His mood was dark by the time he boarded the 747 in Miami that would take him to Lexington. He just found his seat in first class and ordered a drink.

"Welcome home dad," his children sang with glee as they ran to meet Kelley at the gate. "What'd you bring us?" they wanted to know. They were now headed to the baggage claim area in hopes that all of his belongings had survived the trip. Kelley couldn't let his feelings show, but he was paranoid of his surroundings. He hoped he could grab his luggage as quickly as it was unloaded. Once everything was accounted for, the family headed home to Lakeland.

The children settled down for bed, and Adriane went to the bedroom where her husband was preparing for bed. She could now begin her interrogation! "I'm really tired, Adriane," Kelley said. "Can't we just talk about this in the morning?" Then he got into bed and went to sleep.

# Chapter 13

As Christmas neared, the Lake family prepared for the big day as they had in years past. But they all seemed to noticed the affect that Lyn's absence was having on each member of the family.

Gail went through the motions of shopping and sneaking around to hide the presents. She'd also secretly seen her psychiatrist to stock-up on enough pills to get her through the holidays. She'd stopped drinking when others were around, but she continued to indulge herself when she was alone.

Laura missed Lyn terribly. She commented to Gail that if it weren't for her boys, she'd just as soon sleep until January. Then she could wake up and the holidays would all be over. Bobby and Zach were unruly with the anticipation of Santa's arrival and were making Laura a nervous wreck. But, still she seemed to be putting forth an honest effort to work things out with Joey.

"What if we begin some new traditions this Christmas?" Martha asked Gail over the phone.

"I don't want things to be different because Lyn is gone," Gail replied bitterly. "Why do you have to keep trying to make things different? Why do you want everybody to forget Lyn?" she asked with mounting intensity.

"I'm not trying to make anyone forget her. I was just trying to make things easier for you. I want to make Christmas as pleasant as possible for everyone."

"You're always thinking of everyone else, aren't you Martha? Well, I'm sorry, I'd like the whole damned thing to go away. I guess I'm just not as perfect as you are," she declared. Martha quickly excused herself and hung up the phone.

Typical of their relationship over the past few months, Gail would be fine one minute and the next minute she would viciously attack Martha with harsh accusations. Her emotional outbursts had caused quite a strain on what was once a warm and close friendship. The insults, which Martha once overlooked, were becoming harder and harder to ignore. She was hurt and, for the first time ever, she was dreading the Christmas dinner at her house, for fear that Gail would cause a scene.

Mark thought about future Christmases and he daydreamed about how different things would be, one day. He pictured a wife doting on him when he came home in the evenings. Maybe even having another child or two so Emily would have a brother or sister. He bought himself a new art pad and started sketching again, something he had not pursued since high school. He was a little rusty, but the practice was good therapy and it gave him something constructive to do with his time.

Larry was keeping his feelings to himself, but he still tried to spend as much time with Mark as he could. Especially since Joey was spending more time with Laura and the boys. Gail had now become adamant about Mark and Emily staying with she and Larry during Christmas, but Mark insisted that Santa Claus would be coming to see Emily in her own house.

Finally the big day arrived. By mid-afternoon, all of the children made it to Sam and Martha's. Santa had come and gone, leaving exactly what everyone had ordered. Except, of course, a new mommy for Emily. That was a little something that Joey and Laura had kept to themselves. And if Emily was disappointed about not getting a new mother for Christmas, then no one knew it, because she was so thrilled with her new Barbie dolls.

The Christmas feast Martha prepared was fit for royalty. And, being a most gracious hostess, she was able to steer the conversation around anything that might set Gail off. After the meal, the children became loud and rambunctious, so Sam had them put their coats on and play outside.

Bobby wanted to play hide and go seek, and as usual, he got his way. As the older children helped Emily and Zach hide,

Bobby ran to hide behind one of Martha's biggest wisteria bushes in hopes that he would be last to be found. He crouched down where no one could see him and he was very still and quiet as he patiently waited for his cousin Jarrod to count to twenty.

"Eighteen, nineteen, twenty. Ready or not, here I come," he heard Jarrod shout. Then all of a sudden, a distressing sound came from the other direction. Bobby stood straight up, in full view of his stalker. "I see you Bobby," yelled Jarrod. But Bobby took off running as fast as he could go toward the house.

"Daddy, Daddy, Daddy," he ran through the house screaming.

"Slow down, son. What's the matter?" Joey asked grabbing the breathless child up and looking him up and down. "Are you hurt?"

"Something's wrong with one of the horses, Daddy. I heard it makin' an awful sound like it's tryin' to tear down the barn." Joey and Mark were quick on their feet and on their way to the stables with Larry and his brothers right behind them. Sam grabbed his walking cane and was hot on their trail. He knew what the problem was the minute he got within hearing range of the horse snorting and thrashing about in its stall. Those sounds could only mean one thing, colic.

"Isn't he that high dollar stud you boys brought in here last week?" Sam asked Larry as they established where the sounds were coming from.

"Yea Pop," answered Larry, opening the door to the stall. "I guess he didn't handle the trip very well after all."

Mark grabbed the harness on the big stallion as he managed to stand up and Joey fastened a lead line to the harness. "Better call the vet," Sam ordered.

"I'm on it," Mark said as he ran for the phone in the corridor.

Joey led the horse out of the stall and down the hall toward the training track to walk him. "Come on big boy," he said. "Let's try to walk it off." Sam wanted to work with the horse so badly he could taste it, but he knew he couldn't hold up to it anymore. He knew that if he lost his balance under Kingston, he'd likely end up with more problems than just trying to walk without his cane.

"The vet's on his way," Mark announced. Kingston walked a few steps then stopped to paw at his belly. He was in severe pain by now, sweating and pawing at the ground. Joey munched to him to try to get him to walk again, but Kingston sat down, then he slid all the way down on his side and started to roll again. Michael, Phillip, and Sam Jr. started moving things out of his way. It had been quite a while since any of them had seen a horse colic, but they knew how serious it was and Kingston seemed to be getting worse all of the time.

After he rolled for a few minutes, Kingston stood back up. Joey was successful in getting him to take a few steps. Then, down again he went. Everyone stood and watched helplessly while the huge animal flailed about in agony. There was nothing they could do now but wait on the vet and hope.

By the time Dr. Caldwell arrived, Kingston was lying down; head stretched out, and eyes closed. "So sorry to have to call you out on Christmas day, Doc," said Larry rushing to meet him.

"Don't worry about it," the vet said grabbing his bag and hurrying to Kingston's side. "I couldn't hardly believe it when Mark called. You guys haven't had a colic out here in some time."

"We try to do everything we can to prevent it," said Larry. "But, Kingston just joined our family from the "C" Hill Ranch in northern California. And I don't much think the trip across country has agreed with him."

"It sure doesn't look like it," said Dr. Caldwell as he began examining his panic-stricken patient. "Did the previous owner say if he's had a history of colic?"

"No history of it at all," said Larry.

"Well, sometimes it doesn't matter what you do. If they're gonna colic, they're gonna colic. And, that's about all there is to it. How long has he been like this?"

"We called you the minute we noticed him," answered Larry. Kingston held his head up now, but his breathing was laborious and he had a terrified look in his eyes. Dr. Caldwell checked Kingston's pulse. Then he took his stethoscope and listened to the horse's intestinal sounds. When he had completed the exam, he gave Kingston a shot for pain. "I'd like to observe him a little while before I give him anything else. He seems to be calming down a little bit, but it's probably just the medication."

A few minutes passed and Kingston slung his head and stood up. "Whoa fella," Dr. Caldwell said holding his head and stroking a bulge on his side. Kingston looked exhausted, but a little calmer as if the pain was beginning to subside. Joey and Mark took turns walking him up and down the corridor. The sun was down now and the wind was just too cold to take Kingston's already sick body out to the track.

"He's a real beauty," Dr. Caldwell said as he watched Kingston walk back and forth for a few minutes. And Kingston was beautiful. He was jet black without a speck of any other color on him. And he shined like a new penny. The Lakes used to ship in Kingston's frozen sperm for their mares, until they'd finally gotten the chance to buy him.

When Dr. Caldwell was sure that Kingston was under full affects of the pain medication, he decided to give him some mineral oil. "If he's just got a blockage," he said, "I'm hoping this will free it up and we'll be out of the woods. But, I gotta tell you, Larry, I'm worried that during transportation, some of his intestines got kinked up. If he doesn't go to the bathroom soon, we're going to have to take him in for x-rays to find out. My portable x-ray unit is down and I have no way of knowing where the kink might be without taking a picture."

Martha made fresh coffee and Elizabeth helped her pour it into thermoses and take it to the stables. Sam went back to the house when the ladies did. His back and legs had taken about all they were going to. Larry paced back and forth wringing his hands, and everyone else watched, waited, and prayed.

Another thirty minutes went by and still no sign of a freed blockage. "I don't think we need to wait any longer," Larry said. "If we're gonna have to trailer him into town, we need to load him while he's still medicated. I'm afraid he'll hurt himself in the trailer if we don't. Damn, I knew I should have gone ahead and bought that new x-ray machine for the barn."

"I think you're probably right, Larry. If we're looking at a trapped intestine, chances are, it ain't gonna move on its own. In fact, we'd probably better move him while we still can or I'll be doing an emergency surgery right here in the barn."

"Let's get him loaded," Larry said to Mark and Joey. The young men got busy, but Kingston was getting worse again. Joey raised the door at the end of the corridor and backed the trailer in. Mark led Kingston to the trailer, but with fear in his eyes, he balked and wouldn't go in. He backed away and started pawing at his side again. Then he started to snort and paw at the ground shaking his head up and down as if to say, somebody do something to help me.

"Shit," Larry said, as he quickly moved around to the back of Kingston to urge him into the trailer. But he was too late and the horse fell to the ground and started rolling and kicking again. Joey jumped back in the truck to move the trailer out of his way as he painfully thrashed about.

He was suffering terribly, snorting and writhing in misery. He stopped moving long enough to catch a deep breath, then stiffened his legs in front of him. His entire body began to shake violently. Dr. Caldwell grabbed Kingston's head and injected medication into his neck. "Get those blankets," he shouted. "He's going into shock."

Dr. Caldwell started hooking up the IV when Kingston stopped moving and his eyes fixed straight ahead. He took one long, deep breath and held it as Joey and Mark ran back to him with blankets and covered his sweaty body. Then Kingston exhaled. And as he did, his body relaxed.

Larry reached down and closed Kingston's eyes. He'd fought

long and hard, right up to his last breath. But after hours of struggling for his life, he gave up. Kingston had lost his battle.

# Chapter 14

"It happens," Sam said to Martha. "I hate they lost that stallion too, but they've been pretty lucky, all in all. We certainly lost our share in the beginning. Remember?"

"Yes, I remember," Martha said. "It just seems like they've had their share of bad luck this year. I just hope next year is better for them. How did the boys take it?"

"You know Mark. He didn't say a word. Joey is too much like his Mama to keep his mouth shut. He wanted a necropsy done immediately."

"Won't they have to do that for the insurance anyway," asked Martha?

"Yes, but he got a little stirred up about it."

"Well, Sam, he was upset. It's understandable that he'd get a little bent out of shape."

Sam had built one of the finest training facilities of his day, but Larry was convinced that if the Blue Ridge Ranch was going to remain competitive, some additions were going to have to be made. He spent the day after Kingston died reading up on the latest equipment and the most advanced methods of training. He also talked with Dr. Caldwell about the possibility of him coming to work for the ranch on a full time basis. Mark and Joey had been after Larry for a while about implementing a more progressive breeding program and no one in the area knew more about artificial insemination and embryo transfer than Dr. Caldwell.

When Larry gathered his facts and estimated cost list, he pitched the idea to Sam. "Sounds good to me," Sam said, never batting an eye.

"Is that all you're going to say? I thought I'd have a lot of convincing to do."

"You've got to spend money to make money," Sam said to Larry. "And, if Mark and Joey are planning on running the place, then they need to have some input."

"You're right, Pop. I'd like to be able to set them up with everything they need, hire some really good people to help them, and then back off and let them make a go of it. Gail and I are getting ready to travel some and I'd like to still be young enough to enjoy it when we do."

When Larry told Joey and Mark his plans, they couldn't wait to get started. "We can add some bigger stalls on the west side of the barn," Mark said, "and use those two small ones at the end for Dr. Caldwell's a.i. lab."

"Can we finally put in a swimming pool, Dad?" asked Joey.

"Yes," Larry exclaimed. "And, we are going to get rid of that old whirlpool and put in a bigger refrigerated one. And an inside track," he added. They shared all their ideas excitedly and then decided to get their renovations underway as soon as possible. Larry planned to get the estimates as soon as the holidays were over and he could get someone out to the ranch.

He made sketches right away as to how the barn would be laid out. He tried several different methods of adding new wings to the existing barn. Finally he had a design he liked. The new barn would be shaped like a capital H. The existing structure would remain as the center and by adding a perpendicular wing to the west and east ends, the horses could be kept separated, but still they would be under one roof. The center of the H shaped barn would be totally renovated for Dr. Caldwell's office, his laboratory, a x-ray room, a surgery room, and a rehabilitation room, complete with refrigerated whirlpool, and maybe even oversized stalls for the mothers to be.

The east and west wings would consist of a mare barn, a training barn, and a stud barn, all separated by feed and equipment rooms, showers, and offices for the extra staff that would be needed. Larry was quite proud of this arrangement. It appeared to be the most convenient and cost effective approach to take.

He knew he'd be able to coax Dr. Caldwell into coming on board, and not only bringing along his expertise, but also his state of the art equipment. Larry was ready to pay the man whatever he wanted to take over that area of the business, and if the returns were as great as Larry expected they would be, everyone would be able to reap the benefits, including the doctor. He would have his sons set up in a business they could be proud of, and the Blue Ridge Ranch would maintain it's standing in the industry.

Mark was really looking forward to the coming year and all of the ranch improvements. He had something to energize him, something to focus his attentions on. Joey was excited too. Not only were things going better with Laura, now he and Mark had the chance to make a real contribution to the ranch. Joey was tired of feeling like another hired hand. He felt as though he had paid his dues, and he was ready to take on more responsibilities.

Laura decided to keep the books, to become more a part of Joey's life. She was a little nervous about it but she knew Gail would take it slow, and she would never be too far away if she had questions. Laura needed to stay busy. Her heartache seemed to be getting worse with time, not better. Lyn was the first thing she thought about in the morning and the last thing she thought about before she fell asleep at night. "I just need to talk about her," she tried to tell Joey. But, she knew Joey would tell her that she just had the holiday blues. Laura had almost as many unanswered questions as Mark did. And the longer her questions went unanswered, the more they grew and festered inside of her.

"The moving van will be here on the fifth," Adriane told Jason as she hung up the phone. "Do you think you can wait that long?"

"I guess I'll have to," Kelley answered. "I'll call John and tell him when to expect us. We'll just have to stay in the bungalow and store the furniture until we can find a big enough house."

Adriane couldn't believe all the time Jason had spent in Key West and he had not looked at one single house to buy. She hated the thoughts of being packed into an oversized hotel room indefinitely with the children because she knew they would drive her crazy. However, she hated the thoughts of being left behind again in Lakeland even worse.

# Chapter 15

Lakeland City Council went all out for its New Year's Eve "Celebration in the Park". The entire town and many of the surrounding communities turned out to celebrate the new millennium. Sam Lake, being one of the town's oldest citizens, had been asked to say a few words. Martha sat on the make shift stage with him. She was so proud that he'd agreed to do the honors, but she wondered where the rest of her family was. There were game booths set up for the children, fireworks stands, and a band was ready to start playing the minute Sam welcomed everyone and got the party under way.

The park was well lit from the streetlights and booth lights, and Martha gazed out through the crowd that was beginning to gather. She finally caught sight of Joey walking toward the stage. He was holding on to Bobby's hand and Zach was sitting on his shoulders. Mark was right behind them carrying Emily. They were all bundled up and hoping for the snow that had been predicted. Martha guessed that Laura and Gail were probably running late; they were late more often than not. Laura was turning out to be just like Gail, thought Martha.

Jason Kelley didn't want to go to the New Year's bash. He knew the Lake boys would be there. Since he'd been back in Lakeland he'd tried to keep a low profile, but he knew about the rumors that had circulated while he was away. Adriane was insisting that they attend the celebration, even if they could not stay until midnight. All of their children's friends would be there and this would be an event they would remember for the rest of their lives. Jason put up a good argument at first, but then gave in to Adriane. He grabbed his fur-lined parka, thinking that with its hood pulled up, no one could see his face well enough to know who he was.

"Jason, why are you parking so far away from the park?" Adriane asked. "It's just at couple of blocks," he said, "and if we decide to leave before everyone else, we'll be able to get out." Jason was hoping no one would see his car if he parked far away. He was sure the Lake boys knew that he was back in town, but there was no need in adding insult to injury. Jason knew he had to lay low until he could return to Key West. Damn, I bet its eighty degrees tonight in Key West, he thought as he got out of his car and felt the cold Kentucky wind slap him in the face.

The Kelleys made sure their two children were all snug in their coats and hats and they walked toward the park. They were almost to the game booths when the oldest one shrieked; "I forgot my mittens."

"Put your hands in your pockets," Jason said. "We're not going to be here that long anyway."

"But they're in the car, and if I have to keep my hands in my pockets, I won't be able to play any of the games."

"Oh, all right," Jason moaned. "I'll go back to the car and get your mittens. I'll meet you all at that first booth over there," he scowled, pointing at the ring toss. He turned and stomped off toward the car like a spoiled child who'd been told no.

Laura rushed out the door grabbing the keys to the jeep on the way out. She didn't like driving the jeep, but if it snowed she'd be glad she did. It only took a few minutes for Laura to drive from the ranch into town, but she was in such a hurry she missed the turn in to the park. Thinking she'd make the block and come back to the entrance, Laura wheeled into a side street and floored it just as someone stepped off the curb in front of her. She screamed and slammed on the brakes. But, she could not stop in time and she felt the impact of her jeep striking its victim.

Laura jumped out of the jeep and ran to see how badly the

pedestrian was wounded. She knelt down and pulled the hood back away from his face. "Oh my God," she said out loud. Almost petrified with fear, she managed to stand up. What am I going to do, she thought. Laura looked up and down the street to see if anyone saw what happened. Then she pulled the body out of the street and drug it behind some trash cans at the end of the alley. I have to get outta here, she thought, as she stared at the lifeless body. I have to get outta here before anyone sees me. She spun around, climbed into her jeep, and sped away faster than she had arrived.

Laura drove straight to Larry and Gail's house. She was more frightened than she'd ever been in her life. And when she saw Larry's face, she burst in to tears. "Where's Gail?" she bellowed. "I need Gail. Where is she?"

"Gail's gone to the New Year's party at the park," he said. "I don't like that kinda thing myself." Then noticing Laura's disposition, "What's wrong with you? Are you and Joey fighting again?"

"Oh, Larry," she sobbed not knowing what Larry may or may not know about Lyn's affair. "I've just run over," she stopped and took a deep breath. "I've just run over Jason Kelley. I was going to the park and I turned down Jefferson Street and he just walked out in front of me. I've killed him."

"Calm down. Are you sure it was Jason Kelley you hit?"

"I'm positive, I hid him behind some trash cans in the alley."

"Are you sure he was dead?"

"I'm not sure," she snubbed. "He wasn't moving and there was blood on his head. I was so scared, I didn't know what to do. What am I going to do, Larry? What am I going to do?"

"You're not going to do anything," Larry said grabbing her by the shoulders and shaking her. "Calm down. You're not going to do anything and you are not going to say anything about this to anyone. Do you understand me?" he screamed shaking her again. Laura dangled like a little rag doll under Larry's power and shook her head yes. "Now pull yourself together," Larry said and he went outside to assess the damage.

Laura paced back and forth until Larry finally came back into the house and said, "The jeep seems to be okay. Now get back in it and drive back to the park. Don't tell Joey about this," he instructed. "And don't tell Gail either. Nobody needs to know what happened tonight, except you and I."

"But, what about the body?" she demanded to know.

"Don't worry about the body. I'll take care of things from here. Now go back to the park and act as if this never happened."

Laura did as she was told. Driving considerably slower this time, she returned to the park. She found Joey, Mark, and the kids at the concession stand waiting on hot-dogs. "Where have you been?" Joey asked. "I guess when you said you were running late, you really meant it."

"Sorry," Laura said. "The time just got away from me."

"Do you feel all right?" he asked.

"Yea," Laura said. "Why?"

"You're awfully pale looking."

"I'm just cold."

"You look like you've seen a ghost."

As Larry slowly turned down Jefferson Street, he turned off the lights on his truck. Bit by bit, he eased down the street looking for Kelley's body. He saw the trash cans and pulled the truck to the curb, parked it, and got out. He cocked his pistol, steadied himself, and carefully stepped behind the cans. There was nothing there. He looked around for another trash can, but there wasn't another one.

Making his way down the alley, Larry squinted to see in the darkness. Killing Jason Kelley would be the best thing Laura has ever done, he thought. And hell, she couldn't even get that right. He didn't like the thoughts of Kelley still being alive. What if he'd seen Laura? What if he'd made it to the hospital and told someone? The bastard had already caused their family enough heartache. And Larry was not going to let him cause any more.

He crept cautiously through the shadows and searched every dark corner of the alley. He could hear the distant sounds coming from the park. Slowly, silently he tiptoed, looking and listening for any signs of Kelley. Larry reached the end of the alley, so he turned right and started down another street. He jumped as the wind came moaning around the old buildings, thinking it was Kelley. He's got to be here somewhere, Larry thought. Surely he couldn't have gone far. The sound of his own breathing was echoing so loudly in his head that it kept him from hearing the other sounds around him. So Larry stopped, held his breath, and listened. Still he heard nothing. He continued down the street and was almost to the end when he saw something at the edge of the adjoining parking lot.

Jason Kelley managed to crawl to within ten feet of his own car before he collapsed. Larry ran to him and checked his pulse. Damn it; he was still alive. Larry picked him up, threw him over his shoulder, and carried him to his truck. He managed to throw Kelley in the front seat, but what should he do with him next. I know, thought Larry, I'll tie him up and gag him, just in case he regains consciousness. Larry opened the glove box and took out an old cap. He placed it on Kelley's head and leaned him against the door, so it would appear as if Jason was only sleeping.

"It's been over forty-five minutes since your dad went to get those mittens," an irritated Adriane said to her children. "I'm tired of waiting on him. Let's go get them ourselves." The children were elated. It had been all they could do to wait on their dad while the game booths beckoned them to come and play. Adriane held the hand of each child and walked toward the car as she explained what an important lawyer their dad was, and how someone had probably just stopped him needing legal advice. This was not the first time her husband told her that he'd be gone a few minutes but lost track of time.

In her heart, Adriane believed Jason was most likely with some woman and he'd forgotten all about the mittens. She'd had plenty of experience with her husband's continuing interest, no, obsession with the opposite sex. Jason used women to stroke his ego, as if his own self worth depended upon what women thought of him. And when he lost interest in a woman, he'd find another to coerce into giving him whatever he wanted. He would promise them that he'd leave his wife, run away with them, and give them everything they'd ever wanted. Undoubtedly, he was very persuasive; he'd left quite a string of broken hearts behind him.

Adriane knew her husband well. She knew he was not going to leave her. And she couldn't bring herself to leave him, just yet. Their two boys needed their father. Well, this was her excuse, but the truth was, she was comfortable with her country club lifestyle, and her husband provided nicely for her and her kids. Adriane was at the point where she didn't really care what Jason did anymore, as long as there was money in her bank account when she needed it.

She and the boys were almost to the car now, and she was silently cursing Jason for parking so far away. It was dark and spooky and she kept looking over her shoulder, feeling like someone was watching her. Except for the truck that pulled out on Jefferson Street, there was no traffic. Its headlights flashed across them just as Adriane placed the key in the door. The three retrieved the mittens and hurried back to the party.

"Okay Emily" Mark said. "You can ride the merry-go-round one more time, but then we are going to go home." Emily squealed with delight as she, Bobby and Zach rode up and down on their plastic ponies, waving as they went by. It was getting late and Mark wanted to check on Dancer before he went to bed. Her flanks had spread out these past few weeks and she had become very irritable.

"You can leave Emily with us," said Joey. "We're just going to stay a little while longer and we'll bring her home. That'll give you enough time to check on Dancer and you can call me if you run in to anything you need help with. Is that all right with you?" he asked Laura as an afterthought.

She didn't hear him. "Laura," he said louder. She jumped. "What is wrong with you tonight?"

"Nothing," she said defensively. "I'm just tired and cold. Yes, Emily can stay with us if that's what you're asking. You know I don't mind keeping her."

"You just seem like you're in your own little world tonight," said Joey.

"Nonsense," she said. "I'm right here with you."

"Bingo," Gail screamed.

"You won again," exclaimed Martha; "you must really be lucky tonight." Gail would bash people all day long for spending too much time at the horse track, but she'd play bingo till the cows came home. "Well, I'm not doing any good here," said Martha. "I think I'll call it a night and leave it with you young folks."

"Where's Sam?" asked Gail, in between searching for the right letter on her bingo cards.

"He left hours ago. You know he doesn't really care for these things. He just came because the mayor asked him to say a few words to commence the festivities. I'll declare, he and Larry are just alike, just a couple of ole homebodies."

Mark flipped on the lights in the barn and sauntered down the corridor until he came to Dancer's stall. He had been watching her go in and out of false labor all week wondering if this would be the night. He'd seen mares do this before. They'd act like they had a case of colic but it wouldn't last very long. The minute you'd leave them alone, they would get busy. It doesn't take long for a mare to give birth, only a few minutes, if there are no problems, and he was certainly hoping for no problems.

Dancer hadn't eaten very much that night and Mark felt like the time was near. He hesitated to leave the mother alone for very long at a time, just in case something went wrong. He wondered why mares always seem to foal at night. As he started to walk back down the hall to call Joey with a report, he heard Dancer's water break. He quietly, but quickly got back to the stall and watched as Mother Nature went to work. Only a few minutes had passed and the foal was on the ground, struggling and kicking to free itself from the membrane surrounding it. At last, it poked its head out and started breathing.

Man, Mark thought. Joey is going to hate he missed this. He ran back down the hall and this time called Joey. "Are the kids still awake?" he yelled into the phone when Laura answered.

"Yes, we just walked in the door."

"You've got to bring them to the stables," he said. "Millennium Magic has just hit the ground. Dancer is cleaning her up now."

"It's a filly?" asked Laura.

"Prettiest little girl you ever did see."

Dancer meticulously licked and cleaned her baby, and as patches of hair began to dry, it became apparent to Mark that Magic looked just like her mother. She was dark bay/brown, and the lower part of her legs was black. Her mane and tail were black as well, and she had a smidgen of tan coloring on her flanks and her fuzzy little muzzle. But Mark figured this would darken up with age. By the time Joey and Laura got to the stables with the kids, the foal was trying to find her legs.

Dancer backed away from her newborn and waited patiently as Magic tried to stand. Each adult held a child and all six held their breath and cheered silently as she tried over and over again to position her long, spindly legs under her body. Even Bobby was quiet as everyone watched in amazement. At last the filly stood and took a shaky step toward her mother and stopped. She took another rickety step and stopped again. Then, little by little, she carefully wobbled over to her mother and began to nurse.

Mark could see a white streak on the back of her right rear leg now. "Look," he said to Joey pointing it out. "It's that same lightning streak that Dancer has." They could all see it. About half way down her leg, a narrow, jagged streak of white that looked just like a bolt of lightning. "Oh, that's a good sign," he said. "She's gonna be a fast as a bolt of lightning."

Suddenly, the sound of fireworks erupted in the distance. "Happy New Year," cheered Mark.

"Happy New Year," Joey shouted. He led them all outside the stables and turned off the lights. They stood in the darkness and watched the fireworks display a few miles away at the park. The snow was beginning to fall.

Larry drove through the country taking only back roads. He had to stay off the main highway. What the hell am I going to do now, he thought? Kelley was beginning to groan and move around in the seat next to him. He considered all the repercussions that could take place if Laura was charged with hit and run. If only he knew whether Kelley had seen Laura's face or not, but it wasn't worth taking the chance. On the other hand, he could be charged with kidnapping at this point. What was he going to do? Now Kelley was waking up and Larry had to quickly make up his mind.

Kelley rolled his eyes open and looked directly at Larry. "What the hell is going on?" he demanded.

"I'd watch my tone of voice if I were you Mr. Kelley. Do you know what happened tonight?"

"I took my family to the celebration at the park," he said after thinking for a moment. "Where are we? Where are we going? Why is my head bleeding? Are you taking me to the hospital?"

"You're not hurt that bad," Larry said.

"Where are we going?" Kelley asked again. "Why are my

hands and feet tied? What is going on here?"

"I'll be asking all of the questions from now on," said Larry calmly. "Do you know who I am, Mr. Kelley?"

"I, I'm not sure," Kelley replied.

"Do you remember Lyn Lake?"

"Yes, she used to work for me, but I heard she was killed in a car wreck back in the summer."

"Lyn was my daughter-in-law Mr. Kelley." Larry knew the minute the words came out of his mouth he shouldn't have told Kelley who he was. But it was too late to take them back.

"I didn't come back to stay," moaned Kelley. "I'm only here until I can get my business in order and make arrangements for my family. Please, let me go," he pleaded. "I'll leave tonight and you'll never see or hear from me again." Larry turned down another road not knowing exactly what Kelley was talking about, but he didn't have time to ask or even think about it. The roads were getting narrower and the sky was beginning to spit snow at them. Larry had to really concentrate on his driving. "Are you going to kill me?" Kelley whimpered.

"Not just yet," said Larry. "I'm going to leave you here for the night while I make up my mind what to do with you." Larry had driven as far as he could, so he pulled his truck into a clearing. "The rest of our trip will have to be made on foot."

The backside of the Lake's property looked like another world. Nothing there resembled those white-fenced, rolling hills of beautiful bluegrass that covered the front acreage of their property. The backside was mostly rocky cliffs and brush-covered ridges that were of no value to the Lakes since their coal had been mined. And no one had been to the old miner's shack since it was abandoned in the mid-seventies. Even the road that led to the back part of their property had washed away, and the underbrush was so thick, it was almost impossible to walk through. "You can't just leave me out here," Kelley said. "I'll freeze to death, if the bears don't get me first."

"You'll be fine," said Larry as he pulled several horse blankets out of the back seat. He walked around to Kelley's side of the truck and opened the door. Aiming his pistol at his captive's head with one hand, he used the other to untie Kelley's feet and pull him out of the truck.

"You can't just leave me here," Kelley begged. "I'm hurt. I need to see a doctor. I've probably got a concussion."

Larry forced Kelley through the brush and into the shack where he secured him once again. "I'll be back in the morning," he said walking toward the door.

"Please don't do this," Kelley pleaded again. "If you let me go, I promise, I'll leave Lakeland and I'll never tell a soul about tonight. For Christ's sake, I've got a family that needs me. If you won't do it for me, then at least do it for my children."

Larry stopped and glared at Kelley. "Did you think about my family when you were seducing my daughter-in-law? What about my son? Have you thought about him? My wife has aged ten years over the last six months. And how about my granddaughter? She has to grow up without a mother. Have you thought about her? Mr. Kelley, I don't give a damn about your family!"

# Chapter 16

"Yes ma'am, we'll be over this morning to take your statement," the detective told Adriane as he hung up the phone. Jason hadn't always come home when Adriane wanted him to, but she felt there was something different about this time. Once, he had gone back to the office to meet a client on Friday night and didn't show up until Sunday evening. She knew he lied to her, but surely he wouldn't disappoint the boys. Something had to be wrong. Even Jason wouldn't have left his two boys standing there, expecting him to return any minute. She made an excuse for him last night, but what was she going to tell them this morning?

"All right, Mrs. Kelley, I think I have all of the information I need as of now," said Detective Hunter. "I can't actually file this as a missing person report until your husband has been gone for twenty-four hours so let me know if you hear from him. Hopefully, you will. If not, we'll go ahead and get the ball rolling. I am curious about one thing, ma'am," he said.

"What's that?" Adriane asked.

"If you were so concerned about him last night, how come you didn't call me until this morning?"

"I told you, Detective," resenting the implication. "This is not the first time my husband has pulled a disappearing act. It is, however, the first time he's done it in front of the children. He loves his boys, and he would never disappoint them. Now, if you'll excuse me," she said with a condescending air, "I really must go check on them."

Jason Kelley didn't sleep at all that night. His head was still hurting, but mostly he was agonizing over what was to happen next. He was hungry and his blankets smelled like a sweaty horse. He wondered when, or if, Larry Lake was coming back to get him. He's not going to get away with this, he thought. I'll make him pay. The sun was up just enough to light the tiny shack and Kelley looked around in desperation. He could tell, from the way that the light struck the wall, which direction was east. Other than that, he didn't have a clue where he was or how far from Lakeland Larry had taken him. He wished he'd never heard of Lakeland, Kentucky.

Born among Boston's elite, Jason Kelley attended Law School at Harvard University just as his father and grandfather had done. An only child, he was given everything his heart desired. Jason's father divorced his wife and married his much younger secretary after finding out she was pregnant with Jason. They remained married until his father died during Jason's first year at Harvard.

Jason loved his mother and always tried to shield her from his father's indiscretions. But once he left for Harvard, he adopted his father's view of the opposite sex, that women should be kept in the bedroom and out of the business. He married Adriane for the same reason his father married his mother, and their first son was born two weeks after graduation. Jason's mother died of breast cancer before seeing her son graduate or meeting her grandchild.

Jason had no family left, except Adriane and his two boys. He loved his sons, but he never truly found happiness with Adriane. He considered his marriage to be strictly one of convenience. You see, Adriane was the country club type; and Kelley wanted a trophy, a woman that was nothing more than an ornament by his side who would accompany him to prestigious functions. But more than this, Kelley wanted other men to admire him for having such a beautiful wife clinging to his arm. Adriane was well bred, always knowing how to act and what to say. And Kelley wore her well, as he would jokingly tell his associates. Like her husband, Adriane grew up in a small family and she'd lost all her relatives before her children were born. Maybe that's why she stayed with Kelley. They both had no one else.

Jason wanted to practice law in Boston, and the first Boston firm where he'd interviewed called him for a second and even a third interview. He just knew he had the job, but when all was said and done, the firm hired one of Jason's former classmates instead. And when Jason discovered that the candidate chosen over him was female, he was enraged. "If my father were alive, I would have never been treated in such a manner," he bellowed at the senior partner. Jason's behavior was such that he was promptly escorted to the door and blackballed by every respectable firm in Boston.

The interviewing process outside of Boston was not as easy as Jason had anticipated. Without his father or grandfather being there to pave the way, he had only himself to rely on. After almost a year of searching, he joined a small firm in Raleigh, North Carolina and moved his family south. Money had never been a problem for Jason, but timing was. He knew that if he didn't find something soon, it was not going to look good on his profile. Besides, he was going crazy having to spend so much time with Adriane and the baby. He was not ecstatic over the Raleigh firm's offer, but it was a start. Jason knew he'd ruined his chances of practicing law with a decent Bostonian firm and he had to get out and do something before he went insane.

Jason started practicing law with excitement and his career seemed to be getting off the ground. His partners were amazed at how many hours he was able to bill a client for, and Adriane had become a real feather in his cap, since she was getting along splendidly with the wives of his partners. They were finally accepted among Raleigh's socially elite.

But Jason was also getting a lot of attention from his partners' wives. He was witty and charming and usually the life of every party. And like his father before him, Jason had a wandering eye, and was having an affair before he'd been in Raleigh six months.

Of all of the women Jason could have had, foolishly, he desired the boss's wife. And not only did he lose his job when his boss found out, but the scandal threatened his social standing. There was nothing he could do but to start over again in some other town. Adriane was heartbroken over the affair and devastated over the loss of her hobnobbing friends.

When the headhunter called Jason with news of a small firm in Lakeland looking for a lawyer, he was not thrilled to say the least. Lakeland was small, compared to what he and Adriane had been used to. But on the other hand, he wouldn't have to work the long hours he'd worked in Raleigh. And Lexington wasn't too far away, so it wasn't like they were going to be on a deserted island somewhere. The more Jason thought about it, the more Lakeland, Kentucky didn't seem to be such a bad idea.

Now, in the old abandoned miner's shack, Jason could only wish he had it all to do over again. What must Adriane and the boys be thinking? His memory was returning now. He remembered going after mittens. Then he remembered the alley and seeing headlights coming at him. Judging from the pain in his body, he suffered a pretty good lick. The next thing he remembered was waking up in the truck with Larry Lake. Had the Lakes heard he was back in town and tried to kill him? He knew better than to come back to this damned town. What were they going to do next? He had to figure out a way to get out of there.

Larry rummaged through the tack room until he found the broken leather girth he planned to fix months ago. This'll be plenty wide enough to make Mr. Kelley an ankle bracelet he thought to himself. He packed it in his toolbox along with his leather mending kit and plenty of extra rivets. Next, he loaded his battery-powered drill with a freshly charged battery. This, too, he placed in the toolbox on the back of his truck. After locating and loading various other necessities, Larry checked to make sure the log chain was still under the seat. He got in his truck, paused briefly for a mental inventory, and headed for the miner's shack.

Larry was a private person and Gail had learned many years ago that if Larry didn't want to talk, you didn't pressure him to talk. But she knew something was bothering him when she'd gotten up to make breakfast and Larry was already in the barn. She heard him crank the four-wheeler and load it into the back of the truck. It was a beautiful winter morning, and Lakeland was receiving it's first snowfall of the year; so Gail hoped that Larry would be back soon, knowing that the children would get out their sleigh and want to be pulled through the snow.

Larry stopped at the grocery store in town to purchase a gallon of drinking water, a box of crackers, a jar of peanut butter, and a pack of toilet paper. It was still early, and he didn't have to worry about running into anyone that he didn't want to talk to. The snowplows were on the main roads, and he knew he would probably need his four-wheeler to get through the snow and make his way to the miner's shack.

"Looks like you're going to be here a while," he said to Kelley as he entered the shack. "I've brought a few things you'll need. I know peanut butter and crackers are probably not what you're used to, but it'll get you by for a few days."

"What do you mean going to be here a while? How long do you think you can keep my whereabouts a secret?"

"As long as I need to," Larry answered. He went straight to work ignoring everything else Kelley had to say. First, Larry untied the rope that held Kelley's arms to the old iron bed that was shoved into the corner of the main room. Its bedsprings were covered by a dirty, hole-ridden mattress, which had been eagerly chewed by the resident rodents. From the bed, Kelley could see into a small area that must have been a bathroom at one time. There was a hole in the floor, and it probably served as a commode. There was also a broken down table, which by the look of things, had once held a pan of water for washing.

Most mining companies didn't invest large sums of money to construct comfortable bunkhouses. After all, miner shacks were basically used during a shift change. They only served as the supervisor's checkpoint, to make sure that everyone who went into the mine came out at the end of his shift. But more than this, the mining company knew that only a small amount of coal existed on the Lakes' property, so there'd been no point in building anything more than a temporary structure as a miner's shack.

When Kelley's arms and hands were freed, he sat up on the bed, rubbing them and looking at the door behind Larry. He knew better than to think about bolting for the door. His poor health was no match for Larry's size and strength. And he also feared that Larry still had a gun. So for the time being, he would simply do as he was told.

"You can use that hole in there," pointing to the make shift bathroom, "if you need to relieve yourself," Larry said.

Kelley got up and stretched, and then decided he should use the facilities while he had the chance. "Not exactly the Ritz Carlton, is it Mr. Kelley?" Larry laughed and threw Kelley the pack of toilet paper he brought with him. When Kelley was finished, Larry tied him to the bed again, explaining that it would only be for a minute.

Then Larry pulled out the old leather girth and measured Kelley's leg. When he was sure he had the right length, he cut the strap and wrapped it around Kelley's ankle. Being careful to adjust the strap so it was tight enough, yet not too tight, he fastened it using his leather repair kit. Kelley was too scared to put up much of a fight. All he could do was question what was to happen next.

While Kelley was still tied to the bed, Larry drilled a hole into the floor about center of the room. He then measured the log chain to see if it would fit through the hole. Using the drill again, he reamed the hole out a little larger, then slipped the log chain through it and went outside. Kelley could hear Larry crawling around under the floor. He didn't have to see him to know what he was doing.

Once Larry had that end of the chain fixed firmly with an

anchor bolt, he went back into the shack and picked up the other end of the chain. He pulled out all of the slack and walked around the room with the chain in his hand, making sure the chain would reach no farther than he intended. Then Larry made sure Kelley would be able to reach the bed and the facilities.

The only thing left to do now was to fasten Mr. Kelley to the chain. Larry took his tools over to the bed and started working on the strap around Kelley's ankle. When the strap was prepared, he attached the log chain and gave it a tug to check his work. He then released Kelley's hands and told him to stand up and try it out.

"You've got me chained up like a wild animal," Kelley spat.

"I'm not enjoying this very much myself," said Larry. "In fact, I'm not enjoying it at all. Now get up and let me make sure you can get to the john okay."

Kelley stood and stared down at his new ankle bracelet. "I feel like a common criminal," he said, as he moved toward the john, dragging the log chain behind him.

Larry looked around the shack, making sure there was nothing around that Kelley could use to remove the leather strap. "I've got to be going," he then announced. "My grandchildren will want to play in the snow. I'm leaving you this food and water and I'll be back tomorrow."

"Why are you doing this and how long do you plan to keep it up?"

"As long as I need to, Mr. Kelley. As long as I need to."

Back at the stables, Joey and Mark busied themselves getting the sled hooked up to a couple of horses. Sam made the sled himself as a gift to Martha many years ago, and many seasons it had carried the Lakes through the snow. "If that old sled could talk," Sam said as he and Martha came into the barn.

"We'd both be very embarrassed," Martha interrupted. Then Sam winked at her and she giggled back at him like a schoolgirl with a crush.

"How's that new filly?" Sam asked.

"She's a dandy," beamed Mark like a proud father. "Come see for yourself."

"A dandy indeed," said Martha as she peered into the stall. "What are you going to name her?"

"Mark picked out the perfect name," Joey said appearing from around the corner. "Mama Martha, meet Millennium Magic."

"Oh, that's perfect," she said. "And if she can run like her Mama, she's going to be a real winner."

"You boys be sure and get some Vaseline on those horses' hooves before you take them out in the snow," Sam said wisely, knowing it would keep the snow from getting packed up in their feet.

"We will," said Mark. When Joey and Mark came along, it was hard for them not to get emotionally attached to the thoroughbreds, so Sam always made sure there were horses around for them to ride. And he made sure they learned how to take proper care of them. If there was one thing Sam couldn't stand, that was someone abusing or neglecting an animal. Especially a horse.

They could hear Larry driving up outside, and they all walked up the corridor to greet him. "Where you been?" asked Joey.

"I decided to take the four-wheeler in for a good check up, just in case you boys wanted to have some fun with it later," he said. "It needed to have the chain tightened."

"Looks like you might have tried it out yourself," Sam said, noticing the black mud underneath its fenders. "Have you been on the backside of the place?" he asked suspiciously. He knew mud that black could only come from the old mine entrance.

"What better place to try it out?" said Larry.

# Chapter 17

What a way to spend New Year's Day, Jason thought as he lay on the worn-out mattress and piled the horse blankets around him. The sun had just gone down, but he wanted to sleep. The more he could sleep, he thought, the faster time would pass until someone found him, if anyone was looking. He wondered if Adriane was the least bit curious about where he might be, or if she was just accepting his absence, as she had so many times in the past.

He thought of his trip to Key West and fantasized about the life he would have there. Would he ever make it back to his Utopia? John would be expecting him before the week was out, and he wondered if Adriane would call him or not. Then his mind went to the fantastic foods he'd eaten while on the island and he drifted off to sleep.

Shortly after midnight Kelley was awakened by an unfamiliar sound. He kept perfectly still as he tried to figure out what it was he was hearing. It was an eerie, spooky sound that seemed to be getting closer to him. Whatever it was, he hoped it wasn't hungry. Then the sound seemed to surround him. There was more than one. They can smell me, he thought. Hell, I can smell myself. What if they come through the window? He felt like a sitting duck, waiting to be eaten alive. Too terrified to move, he stared at the window until daybreak.

He was glad to hear Larry coming through the woods on the four-wheeler the next morning. He wanted to know what it was that had persecuted him all night. "I brought you some breakfast," Larry said coming through the door with a brown paper bag. He opened the bag and pulled out half a dozen sausage and biscuits and a thermos of coffee. "I hope black is okay with you," he said, pouring Kelley a cup of coffee, then reaching back into the bag for the extra cup he'd thrown in for himself.

"Beggars can't be choosy," Kelley said taking his cup of coffee and holding it in both hands to warm them. Then he took a sip and said, "I heard something in the woods last night."

"What'd it sound like?" asked Larry curiously.

"Like nothing I've ever heard before. It reminded me of an Indian movie I saw once where a young Indian brave was yipping and howling at the moon."

"I saw that movie," Larry said. "It was called Coyote something or other. I don't remember the exact name of it but the brave was named after the coyotes."

"Is that what I heard? Was that coyotes?"

"Probably." Larry handed Kelley a biscuit then reached back into the bag to get one for himself. "There's a lot of coyotes in these woods."

"They surrounded me."

Larry snickered. "I wouldn't worry about them too much. They don't usually attack people."

"What do you mean they don't usually attack people?"

"They've got plenty squirrels and rabbits around here to eat. The only way they would attack a human being is if they were extremely hungry."

"How the hell do you know they won't get that hungry?"

Larry laughed again. "Where are you from, Mr. Kelley?"

"Boston," he said.

"You city boys don't know anything about anything, do you?"

"I do remember reading in the newspaper a few years ago that coyotes were moving into Massachusetts and the other New England states. The article said that there had been such a decline in their food supply that they were being forced to move into other areas. They were killing people's pets and scaring their children."

"That article was probably written by a Yankee. Coyotes get blamed for a lot of stuff they don't do. They're very smart animals. Damned human-like in a lot of ways. Did you know that a coyote chooses a mate for life? And both parents care for their young? Why Mr. Kelley, I guess you could learn something from them, huh?"

Ignoring the implication, Kelley asked, "If they've got enough to eat around here then why were they worried about me?"

"They could probably smell you and thought you were infringing on their territory. All of that yipping and howling was probably to warn the other pack members of danger. They have their own way of communicating, like any other animal. The different barks and howls mean something to them."

"How do you know all that?"

"I was born and raised around here, trapping and hunting. Have you ever been deer hunting?"

"So, I'm not very far from Lakeland then, am I?" Kelley was proud of his investigative questioning.

"You already know the answer to that. If you were very far from Lakeland, how could I be coming and going like I do?"

"Aren't you worried someone will find me?"

"Nope. No one will find you in here, and you could never find your way out. So, city boy, have you ever been deer hunting?"

"No. What the hell do you plan to do with me?"

Larry thought about that question for a minute knowing he had no plans. Then he answered Kelley with, "What do you do when you grow up in a place like Boston?"

"What?"

"What did you do for fun when you were growing up?"

"I didn't do anything for fun when I was growing up. My parents sent me away to an all boys' school. I guess they wanted me out of their hair."

"Didn't you have any brothers or sisters?"

"Not that I know of. How 'bout you?"

"Oh yea. I've got three brothers and one sister. None of them live near Lakeland, but we're all still very close. We grew up riding horses and building tree houses. I can't imagine what it would have been like to grow up without them."

"My father didn't want me in the first place," said Kelley. "And, why in the hell I'm I telling you this? Listen, if it's money you want, all you have to do is name your price. My father left me more than I'll ever manage to spend. You can have it all."

"I don't want your money. In fact, you don't have anything I do want."

"Then why are you doing this? It was you that night in my hospital room wasn't it?"

"You've got nothing I want, I haven't been in your hospital room, and as for the reason I'm doing this, you've got plenty of time to think about it and see if you can figure it out."

Larry stood up and handed Kelley the bag with the rest of the food. "You can keep these for later," he said. "I'll bring you some more tomorrow."

"What, no more peanut butter and crackers?" Kelley said sarcastically.

Larry stared at him. "I'm amused, Mr. Kelley. And amazed too that someone in your position could have such a good sense of humor. Shall I bring his majesty a bottle of champagne with his dinner tomorrow?"

"No, but a clean blanket would be nice. It's cold in here and I smell like a horse."

"Well, I'd certainly hate for you to be uncomfortable. God knows, I want to do everything in my power to see that your stay here is as pleasant as possible." Then he laughed as hard as he could. "You watch out for those coyotes now. I sure would hate for them to get hungry and come back."

Larry left and thought all the way home about his plans. Yea, just what was his plan going to be? And what had Kelley meant by that hospital room comment? Larry had an idea he knew. He just had to figure out a way to find out for sure.

Kelley looked at his watch as the sound of Larry's four-wheeler got farther and farther away until he could no longer hear it. It wasn't even eight o'clock yet. He had never before noticed how loud his watch ticked, but now that it had no competition, the sound seemed thunderous. He ripped it from his arm and threw it across the room. Then he returned to his bed and lay flat of his back staring at the ceiling.

I should have been nicer to him, Kelley thought. Maybe if I'm nicer to him, it'll be harder for him to keep me here. He thought about what it must have been like to grow up the way Larry had. His own childhood kept drifting to the forefront of his mind, but Kelley would shove those feelings back into their closet and close the door before they could escape.

"No sir," Adriane said to Detective Hunter. "I haven't heard a thing from him. It's like he's just vanished into thin air. I don't know what to think."

"Does Mr. Kelley have any enemies that you know of?"

"He's an attorney. I'm sure he has a lot of enemies. Maybe the firm he used to work for would be a good place to start asking questions," she added. "There's something else you should know too, detective."

"What's that?"

"We have plans to move to Key West. The moving van is supposed to be here on Wednesday."

"Any particular reason why you're moving to Key West?"

"Yes. My husband has a history of heart problems. The firm he'll be working with in Key West is much more laid back, and the work is a lot less stressful."

"You might as well go ahead and call the movers and tell them not to come. You don't have to give them a reason. Just tell them it looks like your move has been postponed and you'll call them back when plans are definite. Now then, I'm going to need the name and location of his new employer as well as his previous work history."

Adriane went to the desk and wrote down the information he'd asked for. "Is there anything else you might have forgotten to tell me about the night he disappeared?" Detective Hunter asked. "Anything at all?"

"Well, as you already know, he left the children and I near the entrance of the park. He went back to get our oldest son's mittens from the car. He said he would be right back and would meet us at the first game booth, but he never showed up. As I told you before, I figured that he'd run into someone to talk to and lost track of the time. But, he hasn't called or anything since, and I just know something is wrong."

"I'll see what I can find out for you Mrs. Kelley."

"Will you let me know as soon as you know something?" Adriane asked walking him to the door.

"Same goes here," said Detective Hunter.

The detective got in the car where Brian, his assistant, was waiting. "I have a funny feeling about that woman," he said.

"What do you mean?" asked Brian.

"At first I thought her husband had probably split and didn't want to be found. Now Mrs. Kelley tells me that they had plans to move on Wednesday. I doubt the man would have gone to the trouble of finding a new job and relocating his family if he had planned to skip out on them."

"You never know," Brian said. "People do strange things. Especially Yankees."

"Yea, well, let's get back to the sheriff's office and tell him what we know. Then I want to go talk to Mr. Thaxton and Mr. Sims. I'm anxious to see if there may be more to this moving business than Mrs. Kelley is telling."

"What do you mean?"

"I can't explain it. There was just something about the way she said they were moving that made me think she wasn't really crazy about the idea."

"You're sounding like she's a suspect or something."

"Well, she sure is calm for someone who's worried about her husband. Doesn't it make you the least bit curious when someone says one thing but acts totally different?"

"Yea, I get your point."
"I'll figure it out."

Larry drove straight to Sam and Martha's. He didn't know exactly what he was going to say, but he needed his father now more than he had ever needed him in his life. Sam would know what to do. He always knew what to do.

Martha had already left for the retirement home where she did volunteer work when Larry got there. The timing was perfect, he thought to himself. He didn't want his mother to know what a mess he'd gotten himself into.

"I need help," Larry blurted out to his father, finding him in his recliner watching the news. Sam immediately sat up in his chair and cut the TV off. "I've done it this time, Dad. I've really done it this time." Then, without giving Sam a chance to speak, Larry blurted out, "Dad, on New Years Eve, Laura was in a rush to get to the park, but when she pulled into the parking lot, a man ran out in front of her. Dad, Laura ran over Jason Kelley! She was so scared that she panicked and she drug his body behind some trash cans at the end of the road. She left before anyone could see her and she came to me for help. But I didn't know what to do so I told her to stay put. I decided that I'd pick up his body and dispose of it, but when I found him, Kelley was still alive, and I panicked too. I was scared that Jason could identify Laura, so I tied the bastard up and took him out to the old miner's shack. I didn't know what else to do. I'm sorry, dad, but I couldn't take the chance that Kelley had recognized Laura as the driver of the car that hit him."

Sam was furious. "I thought that son-of-a-bitch left town for good," he said. Then Larry remembered a conversation he'd had with Kelley in the miner's shack. "Dad, a few months back were you the visitor that threatened Kelley in his hospital room? Was it you that insisted Kelley leave Lakeland?"

"It wasn't me," Sam said. "I had someone else take care of it. That just goes to show you, if you want something done right, you'd better do it yourself. Well, he was warned not to come back to Lakeland. I say we just leave Kelley there for a while. As much misery as he's caused this family, it's better treatment than he deserves. And it'll give us time to think about what the hell we need to do with him."

"He says if I'll just let him go he'll leave and never come back again," said Larry. "But, he's a lawyer. There's no way I would trust him to not file kidnapping charges. And, even if he didn't, if he ever figured out who it was that ran him over that night, he'd have Laura on a silver platter. Then where would that leave Joey and the boys? In the same shape as Mark and Emily."

"It's almost unbelievable how this one man has effected our entire family," Sam said. "Just leave the son-of-a-bitch up there for a while. We'll figure out what to do, and in the mean time, he can think about what he's done."

# Chapter 18

"My goodness Mr. Kelley," Larry said, "you're looking a little under par this morning." Kelley's three-day old beard and uncombed hair had him looking more like a hobo than a lawyer. And the dark circles under his eyes were proof that he wasn't sleeping away his time in captivity. "I thought you might want something to read," Larry said tossing Lakeland's weekly newspaper to Kelley.

"So, you brought me the Weekly Reader," Kelley sneered. "Gee, how thoughtful of you. How about a copy of the Wall Street Journal next time?"

"There's something in it that you might find interesting. Check out the front page."

Kelley unfolded the Lakeland Gazette to see his picture plastered right in the center of the front page under headlines reading Man Missing after Millennium Celebration. "Well, I'll just be damned," he said holding the paper at arm's length to get a better look at himself. "Look pretty good, don't I."

The article says the county sheriff's department conducted a thorough search of the park where he had last been seen. It says that foul play is suspected in this case due to information given to them that could not be released at this time. The sheriff is quoted to say; "We plan to follow the investigative guidelines recommended in searches for missing persons in order to ensure that nothing is overlooked and no stone is left unturned."

Kelley continued reading to himself about the clothes he was wearing on the night he disappeared. The article also states his height, weight, and the fact that he has no distinguishing features. Next, Kelley pretended to read aloud to Larry, "If you have any information regarding the whereabouts of Jason Kelley, contact the sheriff's office in Lakeland because, God knows, this county's law enforcement couldn't find their ass with both hands. I could rot out here before they'd find me."

"If you hate Lakeland so much, then why did you come back?"

"I came back to get my family," he replied. "To get my family and my belongings and to move them as far away from this damned town as I can. You don't have to worry. If I ever get out of here, I damn sure won't be back."

"You were told not to come back, this time. And you didn't listen. Here's some food," he said dropping a bag on the floor and kicking it toward Kelley. "I've gotta go."

"You'll never get away with this," Kelley screamed at the door as it closed behind Larry. "Do you hear me? Never!" He retrieved the bag of groceries and sat down on the bed to eat. Then he read the newspaper. Every single word of it.

By the time Larry made it back to the barn Joey and Mark were beginning to wonder where he was. The contractor had been there to look at the plans he'd drawn up, but Larry was no where to be found. "Where've you been?" Joey asked him. "We've been looking all over the place for you. Did you bring the plans?"

"I've got 'em right here," said Larry. "I had some business to take care of this morning and it ended up taking a little longer than I thought it would." He shook hands with the contractor and apologized for his delay. It snowed another four inches during the night, causing Larry's trip in and out of the miner's shack to take a lot longer than it normally would.

Larry rolled out the drawings he'd prepared and spread them across the hood of his truck. He explained in great detail the particulars that he and Joey and Mark had decided on together. Then the four gentlemen walked around the facilities looking and pointing and trying to figure out how they would tie the new in with the old. When the contractor had a clear understanding of what the Lake's wanted to achieve, he rolled the drawings up and took them home to work up a cost estimate.

"Have you noticed how secretive dad has been lately?" Joey asked Mark as soon as they were out of Larry's hearing range.

"Yea, but I just figured it wasn't any of my business."

"Aren't you even curious?"

"Not really," Mark answered. "I don't tell him everything I do and I'm sure he doesn't tell me everything he does."

"I wonder if he and mom are fighting," said Joey. "In fact, I've wondered these past few mornings if he's even sleeping at home."

"What makes you think he's not sleeping at home?"

"Because I get here early enough in the mornings to see that he ain't coming from the house when he comes to the barn. In fact, he's been coming from the opposite direction for the past several days. It makes me wonder."

"Well, if you're that curious, ask him," said Mark. "But, be ready for what you might hear when you do."

"What's that supposed to mean?"

"I just think if he wants you to know, he'll tell you. And if he don't tell you, it's probably 'cause he don't want you to know."

Laura sat patiently as Gail started to explain how registration papers were filed. She wrote down each step that she must use in order to put the information into the computer. "Don't worry about it," Gail told her. "Before long you'll be zipping in and out of this computer like trying on clothes. There's nothing hard about it, once you get used to where everything is."

"Can we take a break?" asked Laura.

"Sure," said Gail. "Do you want a cup of coffee?"

"No. I'll fix me a Coke."

"Is something wrong, Laura?"

"No more than usual."

"What do you mean?"

"When do you go back to the doctor?"

"Next week."

"Do you think your doctor would see me?"

"I don't know. I can ask him."

"I try to talk to Joey about Lyn, but he doesn't want to hear it. I've got to talk to someone, Gail, or I'm just going to explode."

"Well, I'll talk to him for you and see if we can get you an appointment set up."

"I know you think I'm crazy, Gail. I know I should be over it by now, but sometimes I just can't get it off my mind."

"I don't think you're crazy. I'm the same way. It's not just that Lyn died. It's that she left a lot of us in limbo. I've lain awake many nights wondering if she was about to leave Mark and take Emily with her."

"She used to try to tell me that Mark was mean to her and she just about had me believing it. But, not long ago I was at the mall and I ran into some of the girls she worked with. They said they would catch her deliberately walking into doors and putting bruises on herself. Then, not knowing that they had seen her, she would come in to work the next morning and tell them that Mark had hit her. I can't understand why she would do that."

"I can," said Gail. "She was trying to build a case against Mark, so that when she left him for Jason Kelley, she would be able to make it look like it was all Mark's fault. "I'm sure my son was no saint. No man is. But, I don't believe for one minute that he would have hit her."

"We were coming home from shopping one day and she was mad at Mark about something. She told me that she was going to go home and pick a fight with him. She said she knew just the right buttons to push. She was trying then to get him mad enough to hit her. I guess it was so she could justify what she was doing. She lied to me." Laura started to cry. "She lied to me and she used me. And I loved her. She was my best friend and she just used me like she did everyone else."

There was a long pause, and then Gail broke the silence.

"Mark has a date tonight," she said.

"With who?"

"Some girl he met at the park on New Year's Eve. He asked me to keep Emily."

"Well, I'm glad he and Christie are not seeing each other anymore."

"Why?"

"Because she's not Lyn. It just breaks my heart to see him with anyone else."

"You can't expect him to be alone forever."

"I know. But, I don't think I'll ever get used to it. And I know I'll never let myself get close to anyone else like I did her." She took her coke to the kitchen table and sat down with Gail to wait on the coffee to brew.

When the coffeepot stopped sputtering, Gail poured her favorite cup full of the fresh brew and asked, "You ever seen this cup before?"

"Yes," Laura said. "It's your favorite. You've had it ever since I've known you."

"Do you know where it came from?"

"No. I don't guess I've ever heard you say."

"Mark gave it to me for Mother's Day when he was just a little boy. When he thought I was the World's Greatest Mother," she said reading from the cup. She ran her finger over the chipped place in the rim. "There is no greater pain a mother can feel, Laura, than to see her child in pain and to not be able to do anything about it."

# Chapter 19

Clyde Hunter may have been a small town investigator, but he hadn't always lived in Lakeland. He was originally from Kentucky, but he had served many years on the New Orleans police force. He'd ended up taking early retirement after being stabbed six times during a Mardi Gras celebration turned riot. Knowing he was lucky to be alive, he moved his family out of New Orleans and back to the bluegrass country he loved.

The county didn't have much need for a full time detective on its payroll. So Hunter agreed to work for the sheriff's office on a part-time basis, if and when the need should arise for an investigation. He didn't get around as well physically as he once had, but his mind was as sharp as ever. He enjoyed the psychological aspects of a case, getting into someone's mind and figuring out what made them tick. He also took great pleasure in sharing his knowledge. Brian Pratt, a student of criminal justice and part-time deputy, was always eager to learn from and assist Detective Hunter. Even though they didn't work together often, they understood one another well, and they made a great team.

Brian drove the county's only unmarked car toward the Blue Ridge Ranch, while Hunter told him about the things he had learned from the girls at the law office. They'd been happy to oblige the detective's request for any helpful information. In fact, some of them seemed a little too eager to help. It was very plain to see that, not only did Mr. Kelley have the enemies he had put in jail, but he also had a few right there in his own office.

There was one girl in particular that was more willing than others to talk about Kelley's dirty laundry. One evening, she'd returned to the office to pick up some papers and caught Kelley and Lyn together. "Mr. Kelley threatened to fire me if I ever told a soul, but now that he's missing, I'm not afraid to talk," she happily told Mr. Hunter.

Her office had once been located close enough to Kelley's that she could hear his constant arguing with his wife. She then told Hunter, "Adriane was in his office one day, and she was accusing him of the same old stunt he'd pulled in Raleigh. Later, I realized that his wife had been talking about an affair that ended up costing him his job."

These girls weren't surprised to hear of Kelley's disappearance. And they were all quick to point out that a lot of people would like to see him gone. Hunter conducted his questioning while Thaxton and Sims were busy in court, but he had no problem with this. He realized these women were much more likely to "lay it on the line" when it comes to collecting information. "Women," he told Brian, "pay much more attention to the small details. You take that girl back there at the law office. She could probably tell you the exact color and pattern of his tie the last time she saw him, not to mention how many pleats he had in his trousers. The only thing a man would remember is that he had his trousers on. Yes sir, if you can find a woman that'll talk to you, they're much more likely to give you an accurate description."

Brian turned his car down the long driveway that led to the Lakes'. Hunter pulled a notepad from his coat pocket and jotted down Tuesday, January 4th, J. Kelley not a popular man among his law associates. Arrive at Lake Ranch at 11:25 AM.

Joey saw the car pull up outside the stables and walked outside to greet the gentlemen as they stepped out of the car. "Can I help you?" he asked them brushing the dirt from his jeans.

"You can if you're Mark Lake," Hunter replied.

"I'm Joey Lake. Mark's my brother." Then he turned to the stables and yelled out, "Hey Mark. Some man's out here to see ya."

Mark appeared from the barn within seconds. "I'm Mark Lake," he said extending his hand in the direction of Detective

Hunter. Hunter shook hands with Mark and introduced himself. Then he introduced his partner as Brian walked around the car to join them.

"What can I do for you?" Mark asked.

"We'd like to ask you some questions," Hunter said

"Shoot. I'll tell ya anything ya wanna know."

"How well do you know Jason Kelley?" the investigator started.

"I've never met the man," said Mark.

"You've never met him?"

"Nope. I've never met him. And frankly, I hope I never do. My wife used to work for him. But, I'm sure you already know that or you wouldn't be here asking me questions. Have you also been told that she was having an affair with him when she died?"

"Yes I have," said Hunter. "And I'm sorry to have to ask you some of these questions."

"That's okay. We've all got a job to do. And you're just doin' yours. I saw in the paper where he's missing. And I don't mind telling you I hope the son of a bitch is dead. But, I've never met him. And if you're here to find out if I know anything about his whereabouts, I don't."

"Have you ever met him?" the detective asked looking at Joey.

"No sir, I can't say that I have. We don't exactly run with the same group of friends if you know what I mean. But, I'm different from Mark. I'd like to meet him. I'd like to whip his ass."

"Where were you boys on New Year's Eve?"

"That's easy," Joey said. "We were at the celebration in the park."

"Both of you?" Hunter asked Mark.

"Yes sir."

"Do you have anyone that could vouch for this?"

"Only the whole town. We must have talked to two dozen

people before the night was up."

"What time did you get there?"

"Well, I remember picking Joey and the boys up about 8:30 so it must have been about 8:40 or 8:45."

"Who are the boys you're talking about?"

"Joey's kids, Bobby and Zach. I had my little girl with me."

"Are you divorced, Joey?"

"No, my wife met us there. She was running late getting ready. She's always late."

"I know what you mean. I have a wife of my own. And what time would you say she met you there?"

"Uh, she was probably about an hour behind us. She would say she wasn't that late, but I think it was probably an hour."

"Did she come alone?"

"Yea."

Then looking back at Mark, "What time did you leave to go home?"

"I'm not sure exactly. It had to have been some time between 11:00 and 11:30."

"Did you go straight home?"

"No sir. I came straight here. I had a mare due to foal at any time and since we don't have a full time vet yet, I was watching her pretty close. But that's fixin' to change."

"What is?"

"We're gettin' a full time vet."

"Oh. Well. That's good. Now, anyway. Did anyone know where you were?"

"Yea, Joey and his wife kept my girl with them so I could come by and check on her." Then with growing enthusiasm, "She dropped one too. Right before midnight. I called them as soon as she hit the ground and they came over to see her. We named her Millennium Magic. Would you like to see her?"

"Why, yes. Yes I would," Hunter said, surprised to be asked.

Brian and Hunter followed Joey and Mark to the stall where mother and filly stood in all of their glory. "Ain't she a beaut?"

Mark beamed.

"I'm quite impressed," Hunter admitted.

"She's gonna be a real runner too," Joey said. "You wouldn't happen to like to place a little wager now and then would you Detective Hunter?"

"I am from Kentucky," he said smiling.

"Well, you just remember where you saw her first."

"Thanks for your time boys, but I guess Brian and I better be gettin' on back. If I think of anything else I want to ask you, I'll let you know."

"Okay, but can I ask you a question?" Mark said.

"Sure."

"Don't you think he might have just run out on his old lady? I mean, they aren't exactly a match made in heaven."

"All I can tell you is that right now, it's too early to rule anything out. But thanks again for your cooperation."

"What'd ya think?" Brian asked as the two got back into the car and headed back down the driveway.

"I really don't think the boys have anything to hide," said Hunter. "But, like I told Mark, it's too early to rule anything out." They met Larry turning in the driveway as they pulled out onto the main road.

"Who was that leaving the ranch?" Larry asked when he got to the barn.

"A detective Hunter," Joey answered. "He's investigating the disappearance of Jason Kelley."

"Really," said Larry. "What made him think he'd be here?"

"He didn't think he'd be here," Mark said. "He just wanted to ask us some questions."

"What kind of questions?"

"Where were we the night he disappeared? When did we get to the park? When did we leave the park? Just stuff like that. He said he'd be back if he thought of anything else that he needed to ask us."

"He's probably done messed with the wrong person and

somebody's shot him," said Joey.

"If that's the case," Larry added, "then he got what he deserved."

"I don't figure he's dead," said Mark. "I bet he's just run out on his old lady, or maybe she had him knocked off. Yep, my bet is on the wife."

"I've got a hundred-dollar bill that says when they find him, he's dead," said Joey.

"You're on," Mark said. "You want in, dad?"

"No. I just want to get back to work and finish up so I can go to the house. I haven't been sleeping very well and I'm tired." Joey gave Mark an "I told you so" look and they headed back to work.

Larry slipped back to his truck to call Sam. "Dad," he said into the phone, "Do you know a Detective Hunter with the county sheriff's office?"

"I know of him," Sam answered.

"Well, he's been out here at the barn snooping around. He's been asking the boys all kinds of questions about where they were the night Kelley disappeared."

"Is that right?"

"I wasn't here when he came by, but he seemed to have been directing most of his questions at Mark."

"Well, don't worry about it. I probably need to have a talk with Bill anyway." He hung up the phone, then immediately picked it back up and dialed the sheriff's office.

Bill Williams had been county sheriff for the past sixteen years. Sam's support not only helped Bill get into the sheriff's office, it played a big part in keeping him there. Sam thought Bill to be a very fair man. But it was time he called off his dogs.

"I'll take care of it," Bill told Sam over the phone. "I told Hunter to follow whatever leads he felt were necessary, but I had no idea he was headed out to your place."

"Mark's had a hard enough time over this whole Lyn thing," said Sam. "And, you know as well as I do, he don't have anything to do with this horse shit."

"No problem, Sam. How 'bout you lettin' me buy you a cup of coffee some time?"

"Sounds good to me."

"Better yet, why don't you meet me at the café in the morning? I'll buy your breakfast. How's eight o'clock sound?"

"Great. I'll see you then."

"I heard you and Brian stopped by the Lake place this morning," Bill said to Detective Hunter before he left to go home.

"Yea," Hunter said.

"I don't think there's much need in wasting the tax payers money out at the Lake place, Clyde."

"You're right. After I went by the law office, I decided Mark Lake had as good a reason as anybody to want to see Kelley gone. But after I talked to the boys, it was clear to me that they have nothing to hide."

"That family has been about as good to me as my own," the sheriff said. "I sure would hate to see them get drug into something they had nothing to do with."

"I understand."

"It's been a long day, Clyde. I'll see you tomorrow."

"One more thing before you go, Bill."

"What's that?"

"Has this case been filed with the National Crime Information Center?"

"No."

"Isn't it routine procedure to list all missing persons with the NCIC?"

"No it isn't," he said bluntly. "It's up to my discretion. And for right now, I think we need to just continue with our investigation as is. We don't need the feds coming in here and sticking their nose where it don't belong. They always screw things up when it comes to investigating in a small town. There's too much gossip here and they can't recognize it and weed out what's real from what's rumor. I guess they have their place, but I'm not so sure a town like Lakeland is it. Besides, we're not even sure a crime has been committed. A missing person is not a crime."

"You have a point there."

"Right now we need to try to pinpoint exactly what it is we're investigating."

"What are you thinking, Bill?"

"Well, there's been no ransom note. There's been no physical evidence of a struggle. Hell, a grown man is not abducted as easily as a woman is or child would be. I guess if he's been napped, there'll be a clue somewhere if we just look hard enough to find it."

"But you don't think he's been napped, do you?"

"It really doesn't look that way. The man made enemies everywhere he went. I know we can't rule it out, but frankly Clyde, I feel like we're just looking for a body at this point."

"You're right. It doesn't look like he's just skipped the country, either. A man getting ready to move his family? No gambling debts at the tracks he's running from. It just don't add up that he's hid out somewhere. That don't even fit his personality profile."

"Well, this is a small town. And, sooner or later somebody will talk if there's anything to say. But for right now, we've got to keep our minds open to every possibility. I tell ya, that James Thaxton is normally a pretty sharp man, but he sure screwed up when he got Kelley to come in here. Hell, I don't like him either." Then with a chuckle he added, "But you know, if you put together a list of all the people who don't like him or who might like to see him dead, you'd probably have more leads than you could shake a stick at. You wouldn't know where to start."

Hunter laughed. "Have good evening," he said. "I'll see ya tomorrow."

"You too."

It was only a few minutes past 5 o'clock, but it was already dark and Kelley spent another long, cold day alone. He had eaten all of the food Larry brought that morning and was hungry again. Not really hungry, he thought, just bored. Knowing he had to keep his strength up, he got on the floor and started doing pushups. Next he did a few sit-ups, and then some jumping jacks, but they were hard to do because the chain attached to his ankle.

Kelley flopped down sideways across the bed and wondered how long could this go on. Subconsciously, he awaited the coyotes. Now that Larry had explained their bizarre way of communicating, he was no longer scared of the sounds. In fact, he felt strangely close to them. They had been his nightly companions, as curious about his presence as he was about theirs.

Then it hit him. If coyotes can survive out here, then I can too. What would the Indians have done in this situation? There has got to be some means of escape. There's got to be some reason they're keeping me alive. Larry would have killed me already if that was his plan. He's keeping me around for some reason, but what?

Kelley heard the yipping of his coyote friends announcing their arrival, and he didn't feel quite so alone. "Hello," he said. "I was wondering when you would get here." Maybe Larry Lake is trying to drive me insane, he thought. Well, I refuse to give up. I'm like the coyote, a survivor. I'm sly as a fox. I'm in control of my own destiny. I can't count on anyone finding me so I'll have to rely on myself. I'll try to get as much information out of Larry as I can. Yea, that's it. I'll get him to talk. If I can figure out what makes him tick, maybe I can talk him into taking off this chain, then I can follow his tracks out of here. Kelley's thoughts turned into dreams and his dreams into nightmares.

He saw his two sons holding hands and walking down the streets of Lakeland. They walked and walked until they reached the entrance of the park. "Daddy," they screamed. "Daddy, where are you?" He yelled back at them, but they couldn't hear him. They wandered around aimlessly searching for him. "Daddy," they screamed again. "We don't need our mittens, Daddy. Just come home. We don't need our mittens."

# Chapter 20

Mark lay on the couch staring up at the ceiling, knowing it was time to get up but not wanting to. He really had a good time with Kathy last night. When his cousin had introduced them in the park, he had not wanted to meet anyone. He was just beginning to get used to the idea of being single. He certainly wasn't ready to invite anyone else into his life. But, he liked her. More than he had intended to.

Kathy had a certainty about her. A self-confidence that Mark was intrigued by, even a little envious of. She was smart, but easy to talk to. He could learn a lot from a person like this, and he definitely wanted the chance. He'd asked her out again before their first date was over, just to be sure she was having the same feelings.

Although Mark didn't realize it at the time, he felt guilty. He was unaware that guilt was simply another phase of grief, so he shoved the unfavorable thoughts of Lyn back into a dark corner of his mind. He didn't want to face these feelings head on, nor deal with the unpleasantness they might bring. Mark felt guilty because his marriage was not a happy one, and to a certain degree, he felt responsible. He was happier now than he'd been in a long time, in a relieved sort of way, and he felt guilty for that too. Every aspect of his life, be it good or bad, left him with some depth of guilt.

When he was alone, Mark drank to keep his feelings locked away. He also started getting high with some of the guys that hung out at Marty's Place. But, by subconsciously postponing the inevitable, Mark's emotions were healing like a puncture wound that scabs over on the outside, but is infected and festering underneath. Until he admitted this to himself, he would never be free from his past.

Mark got up and took a shower. He then made his way to the kitchen to make cheese toast, Emily's favorite breakfast. "Emily, wake up, honey. Breakfast is ready." Emily ate a hardy breakfast then dressed for daycare. It was Mark's usual routine to drive his daughter to the daycare center, and then he would head to the stables to begin his day.

"Good to see you Bill," Sam said, walking up to the booth where the sheriff was seated. Bill stood to shake Sam's hand, then sat back down and watched as the good-hearted old cuss plopped down and started wiggling around in his seat trying to get his feet untangled. "Damn legs just don't move as good as they used to," he said. "I stagger around like I'm drunk half the time. Not that I'm against it you understand, but it is a little early in the day."

Bill chuckled and shook his head as Katie strolled through with her usual good mornings and filled coffee cups for each of them. "How are things going out at the ranch," Bill asked?

"Fine, fine," Sam replied. "The boys lost a stallion on Christmas Day, but business is good, and no matter what ya do, you're gonna lose a few. Larry's in the process of getting quotes on a face-lift for the old barn, and Joey and Mark are like two kids waitin' on Christmas Day all over again. They want to get all of the latest equipment and really do her up right. I guess if it's gonna be theirs, then they need to fix it like they want it. But, that's enough of that horseshit. What do you know?"

"Well, there's not just a whole lot to tell, Sam. Clyde Hunter is looking into the disappearance of Jason Kelley, which you already know. He's not worried about Joey or Mark having anything to do with it. He just has to talk to everyone. The more questions he can get answers to, the more successful he's going to be at finding him."

"I'd rather have him looking into it than the damned FBI snooping around Lakeland. The last time the federal boys were in town for something, they ended up causing more damage than they did anything else."

"I know. I'm of the same opinion. And, I've already taken care of it with Detective Hunter. I expect that he'll be about as thorough as a man can be, though. He don't have anything else to focus his time on, except huntin' and fishin'. He's come back here from New Orleans to retire, and from what I've heard, he always gets his man."

"I heard he got cut up pretty bad during Mardi Gras a few years ago."

"I swear, Sam. Nothing gets past you, does it?"

"Not if I can help it. So, from the inside, what does it look like to you?"

"It's too early to lean in one specific direction. Could be just about anything from homicide to a man who skipped out on his wife or the bill collectors."

"I sure would like to be kept informed of any new developments."

"No problem, Sam. I'll let you know, as more evidence becomes available." Katie came through and took Sam's breakfast order of one egg, one piece of toast, and two strips of bacon. Sam had never been a big eater. He'd eaten this same breakfast every morning since he was a young man. Bill, on the other hand, ordered a tall stack of hotcakes with eggs and a side order of ham. Then, turning back to Sam he said, "Kelley's wife told Detective Hunter that they were planning to move to Key West. In fact, the moving van was to suppose to arrive today. But now that Kelley's disappeared, she's not allowed to leave town."

"Key West is a great place to visit, but why would anybody in their right mind want to live there?"

"Supposedly Kelley's had some heart problems, and they were looking for a more laid back type of atmosphere."

"Is that right?" said Sam.

"Yea, I think Detective Hunter will probably be going down there to see what he can find out."

"That's probably a good idea. Let me know if he finds anything."

They finished their breakfast, and sure enough, by the time Bill made it to the office, Detective Hunter had already filled out an expense request form for a trip to Key West. "When do you want to leave?" he asked the detective as he added his signature of approval to the bottom of the form.

"I plan to fly out of Lexington first thing in the morning so I can be down there by noon. I don't look to be gone for more than just a few days. He'll either be there or he won't."

Larry was moving slow this morning. He'd spent another night tossing and turning and worrying about what would happen next. Not knowing was driving him crazy. Although that wasn't necessarily a bad thing because, if it was driving him this crazy, then Jason Kelley should be on the brink of insanity by now. He knew his father was right. In time, they would figure out what needed to be done, but for right now, he had to play it cool. He couldn't afford to make any mistakes.

He was later than usual arriving at the miner's shack, and Kelley was awake and waiting on him. "I brought you some more water," Larry said. "And there's all kinds of food in the bag."

"Is this Wednesday?" Kelley asked.

"Yep."

"I'm supposed to be moving today."

"Yea, I heard."

"Friday is my son's birthday. I'm going to miss my son's birthday," he whimpered.

"What a coincidence. Lyn missed her daughter's birthday." Larry remained very calm as he went about his business checking Kelley's ankle bracelet. Then, out of the blue he asked, "Were you talking to Lyn on the phone when she wrecked the car?"

"What ever gave you that idea?" asked Kelley.

"The phone bill."

"What if I was?" he taunted. "She did work for me."

"What did you hear?"

"What do mean, what did I hear?"

"What did you hear when Lyn wrecked the car and was killed?" He asked more specifically.

"I heard a crash and then the phone went dead," Kelley said with no emotion what so ever.

"It doesn't bother you?"

"I try not to think about it."

"Is that the way you live with yourself? You just don't think about all the hell you've caused other people? I wish you had to hear that crashing sound over and over and over again. And I wish you could see what I see when I close my eyes and try to sleep." With that, Larry walked to the door and opened it. Then looking back at Kelley he added, "And I hope you burn in hell." He slammed the door behind him and was gone.

Kelley stared blankly at the door. Memories of Lyn started to creep to the forefront of his mind. But he pushed them back and quickly replaced them with thoughts of the hospital and how scared he had been the night the visitor came. "They're going to kill me," he said out loud. "I don't know what they're waiting on, but they're going to kill me."

Larry stopped back by the house before going to the barn that morning and Gail met him at the door. "I've got everything planned," she announced with delight. "We can fly out next week and spend the rest of the month in Hawaii. I was able to rent the same little bungalow on the beach we had last time. I've already made the reservations. The only thing left to do is finalize the plane tickets."

"I can't go that soon," Larry said knowing he couldn't leave until something was done with Kelley.

"What the hell do you mean you can't go that soon? You told me to plan the trip and make the reservations. That is exactly what I did. And now you tell me you can't go that soon?"

"I'm sorry, Gail. If you'd just give me a few weeks to get the barn renovations underway, then we can go."

"To hell with those renovations. Let Joey and Mark take care of them. You're the one who's always saying they're grown, leave them alone. Well, they're grown. So, you leave them alone. They can manage fine without you. Honestly Larry, I don't know what has gotten in to you. I did exactly what you told me to do and now you're backing out." She picked up her Bloody Mary and stormed out of the kitchen.

"What's gotten in to me?" he screamed after her. "Has it dawned on you that maybe I might need more than a weeks notice? Or do you stop to think about what anybody else needs these days?"

Joey was standing outside the kitchen door hearing every word they said and decided that this was not the best time to go in. He headed for his truck and drove straight to the barn to tell Mark what he'd just overheard, but he walked in the tack room just as Mark lit up a joint. "What the hell are you doing?" he said fanning a puff of smoke out of his face.

"I'm looking for that big swivel hook that used to hang right up there," he said pointing at the pegboard they used to hang tools on. "Have you seen it?"

"That's not what I meant, Mark. What the hell are you doing smokin' a doobie?"

"Aw, man. Don't get up on your damn soapbox. It clears my head and helps me deal with shit. Besides, it don't give me a hangover like drinkin' does."

"It's illegal too. You forgot that."

"I ain't gonna get caught with it. I don't even buy it. This is just some a friend gave me the other night."

"I think you've lost your freakin' mind. I think the whole damned family has. Dad's drinkin' like hell and Mom's eating pills like they were candy. And last night I find out she's got Laura an appointment with her shrink so I guess she'll be the next one hooked on somethin'."

"I think you're overreacting."

"You think so? I happen to think I'm the only one left

around here with any sense at all. Me and the horses." He grabbed up everything he needed for the exercising arena and left Mark standing in a cloud of smoke.

# Chapter 21

Clyde Hunter arrived in Key West the next morning and took a cab from the airport straight to John Forbeson's law office. He had no intentions of being on the island any longer than he had to. But, when he got there, what he found was a locked door and a sign that said, "Back at 1:00". He decided to walk down to the famous Duval Street and see if he could find a cup of coffee and a sandwich.

It reminded him a lot of New Orleans on a smaller scale. He stopped at a sidewalk café and sat down to look at the menu. When the waiter finally appeared, he ordered. Then as an afterthought, Hunter showed the young man a picture of Kelley, hoping he might remember him.

"I'm sorry Mister. I see a lot of people. I don't know if I've ever seen him or not," was the young man's reply.

"Thanks anyway."

Then sensing Hunter's frustration, the waiter asked, "Is he gay?"

"I don't think so, but I wouldn't guarantee it," said Hunter. "Why?"

"Because if he's not, it would narrow your search down to only certain portions of the island." Then he picked up a napkin and wrote down a list of establishments that Kelley would be avoiding if he were straight.

"That would save me a lot of time. Thanks."

"No problem," the waiter said. "I'll be right back with your order."

Hunter knew if he was going to find anything out about Jason Kelley, he was going to have to stay the night and hit the bars. Detective work is a young man's game, he thought to himself. He did not relish the idea of hopping from bar to bar flashing Kelley's picture around and asking probing questions of those who probably wouldn't be nearly as helpful as this young man had been.

He took his time with his sandwich, then left the waiter a very nice tip, and walked through some of the specialty shops while he waited on 1 o'clock to arrive. He bought a map of the town, some hard candies, and a book on gun collecting to read on the flight back to Kentucky. Finally, it was time for him to head back to the law office.

Good, he thought, as he crossed the street in front of Forbeson's office and noticed that the sign had been removed from the door. He turned the doorknob and hesitantly entered an extremely casual looking reception area. "Be with you in just a minute," he heard a voice call from the back. So he tried to make himself comfortable on a wicker sofa and started thumbing through his new book, growing increasingly impatient and ill at ease the longer he was made to wait.

Finally, a man appeared from the back wearing a pair of cut off bluejeans, a tee shirt, and a worn out pair of sneakers. "Sorry I kept you waiting. I'm John Forbeson," he said, extending his hand.

Hunter stood and shook his hand. "I'm Clyde Hunter," he said pulling his credentials from his pocket and flashing them at Forbeson. "I'd like to ask you a few questions."

"Come on back," said Forbeson, leading the way down a hallway and into his office. "Have a seat and tell me what I can do for you."

"I'm trying to locate Jason Kelley," Hunter said. "His wife told me that he was coming to work for you, but he's been missing since New Year's Eve. Do you know anything of his whereabouts?"

"That's strange. He was here and yes, he has planned to join my practice. I kept expecting to hear from him regarding his arrival date, but I never did. I didn't think that much of it, though. I figured he might have run into problems with the movers because of the holidays."

"So, he has not been in touch with you since he left?"

"No. I thought I'd give him a few more days and if I didn't hear from him, I was going to give him a call to make sure he hadn't changed his mind. I had no idea he was missing."

"Is there a possibility he could be in Key West without you knowing it?"

"I suppose a slight possibility, but I doubt it."

"Think back for me, Mr. Forbeson. Do you recall anything he might have said while he was here that would lead you to believe he was about to leave his wife?"

"No. He was going to discuss the job with her, but he was already pretty much counting on taking it. He really seemed to like it here."

"Did he mention any enemies he might have to you?"

"No. He said he was tired of the rat race, tired of the stress. In fact, he said he'd be happy if he never set foot in another courtroom."

"What about other people he met while he was here? Do you think they might have been in contact with him?"

"I don't know, but I'd be happy to show you around and introduce you to the crowd he ran with. He liked to party down at the waterfront. How long do you plan to be in town?"

"It depends on what I find. Not long, I hope."

"Well, there's never much that goes on around here this time of year so I'm pretty free right now. What do say we get started?"

"Sounds great." Hunter was indeed grateful for the help. The people did seem to be much friendlier here than in New Orleans. Forbeson excused himself to make a few phone calls then hung the closed sign back on the door and locked up. They walked down to the waterfront where Hunter found a room for the night and checked in. Now they would go door to door, showing Kelley's picture and asking questions. The owner of the chalet that Kelley rented while he was in town remembered him immediately, but had not seen nor heard from him since he'd checked out a few days before Christmas.

"I'm bushed," Hunter told Forbeson. "I guess I'm not as young as I used to be. What time do the bars get cranked up?"

"It'll be eleven or twelve before the night crowd gets going."

"Then let's get a bite to eat while we're waiting. I could use a nice cool place to sit down. There was snow on the ground when I left Lakeland and my body was not ready for this eighty-eight degree weather."

The Thursday night crowd was already beginning to gather back in Lakeland at Marty's Place. "I'm sorry I got so pissed off at you yesterday," Joey said to Mark as they pulled up outside the bar. "It's just that nothin' is the same. Everything has changed since Lyn died. Mom and Dad are at each other's throats constantly and Laura cries all of the damned time. You can't go off the deep end too. I don't know what I'd do if I didn't have you to talk to."

"I ain't goin' anywhere," said Mark. "I just need to clear my head sometimes. It's helped since I've bought all new furniture for the house and got rid of all Lyn's stuff, but there are some things I can't erase by making the house look different. Sometimes I get things on my mind and I can't deal with 'em without a drink or a smoke."

"Maybe if we talked through all those things it'd help."

"I can't come runnin' to you every time things get me down, Joey. You've got Laura to deal with."

"You're gonna have to be able to talk to somebody. What about Papa Sam?"

"I don't know. I hate to worry him. I've been thinkin' about goin' to see Elizabeth. She told me I could come up there anytime I needed to get away for a while."

"Then go. A change of scenery might do you good."

"I might. Right now I just want to go in and get a beer."

"Hello," Laura said into the phone quickly. She had Emily scooted up to the dining table with the boys trying to get them to eat dinner when the phone rang.

"Well hello good lookin'. It's been a long time since I've heard that sweet voice of yours," the caller's voice dripped with cynicism.

"Mike? What are you doing calling here?" she whispered.

"Well it's been so long since I've heard from you, I thought you had forgotten about me. Aren't you glad to hear from me?"

"What if Joey had answered the phone?"

"I just saw Joey and Mark going into Marty's Place. I knew he wasn't going to answer the phone. What's the matter, babe? Haven't you missed me? Can't we get together?"

"No," she blurted. "I can't. Things are different since Lyn died."

"Why should things be different between us? Look, it's been months and I've given you time. But, I miss you and I need to see you."

"I said I can't. Joey would kill me if he knew about us. Please, don't call me again." She slammed the phone down and returned to the table where the children were showing out for each other.

"Stop it," she spat at Bobby. "Get your finger out of you nose and eat your dinner." The children quieted down and started to eat, but Laura looked at her plate and felt sick to her stomach.

"What the hell?" Joey said turning around from the bar just in time to see Mark send some guy flipping backward over a pool table. "Wait for me," he screamed not knowing what he was fighting for but determined not to be left out. He ran across the room and jumped on another dude just about to take Mark from behind. With one swing, he split the guy's lip open and knocked him to the floor.

Mark didn't notice the skirmish going on behind him. He dove on top of his opponent and was banging his head against the floor. Then others joined in the free for all, and before Marty knew it, the whole bar was a war zone. Fists were flying, furniture was being overturned and bets were being placed on the side. It'd been quite a while since Marty had seen a brawl this good so he stood back for a few minutes and let the boys blow off a little steam. But when somebody's tooth came sliding down the bar toward him, Marty decided that it was time to call the law.

"Sam, Bill Williams here. Sorry to bother you this late, but I couldn't get an answer at Larry's."

Sam had fallen asleep in his easy chair and Martha thought he looked so comfortable that she'd left him there and went on to bed. "What's the matter?" he asked almost dropping the phone.

"I've got Joey and Mark down here at the jail. They're all right; they've just had a little too much to drink and I thought you might want to come get them."

"I'll be right there," Sam said. He stood up and got his balance, then went upstairs to tell Martha he'd be back in a few minutes.

A few minutes later he walked into the sheriff's office and found his grandsons sitting in a cell staring back at him through blood-shot eyes. "Apparently, someone down at Marty's said something about Lyn and Laura that the boys didn't like," Bill said.

"That's gonna be a beaut' come mornin'," Sam said to Joey, whose right eye was almost swollen shut.

"You should've seen the other guy," Joey said with a bloody grin.

"You can tell me all about it when you've sobered up some. How much do I owe you Bill?" Sam asked the sheriff reaching for his wallet.

"Don't worry about it, Sam. But, you or Larry might want to check with Marty tomorrow. The place was pretty much a mess by the time I got there to break things up."

"I'll do that, Bill. I appreciate you calling." He loaded the boys into his truck and drove toward the ranch. "You boys want to go to my house and get cleaned up before I take you home?" he asked.

"No," said Joey. "Surely the kids will be asleep by now."

"Just drop me off at Joey's too," Mark added. "I'll just crash there tonight."

Laura already had the children in bed by the time Joey and Mark staggered in, but she was still awake and pacing the floor. She hadn't heard from Mike since the week before Lyn died and she hoped to never hear from him again. Why the hell would he be calling now?

"What happened to you two?" she asked when she saw them.

"Just a little scuffle my dear. No real harm done," Joey snickered as he tried to hug her close to him.

"Oowie, you stink," she said pulling away from him. "What have yawl gotten into?"

"Come on baby. Give me just one little kissy," Joey said jokingly.

"That ole Mike Keys and some friends of his came in Marty's tonight and started mouthing off a bunch of stuff about you and Lyn," said Mark.

"What kind of stuff?"

"Not so nice stuff," Joey said. "Stuff you don't need to hear repeated."

"I have a right to hear it, if it was said about me," she demanded.

"No you don't," said Mark as he flopped down on the couch and kicked off his boots. "You don't mind if I crash here, do ya?"

"You two are unbelievable. Is there anything yawl can't find to get in to?"

"We don't know yet," said Joey as he headed up the stairs. "We're still young."

"Joey Lake, you better just go straight to that shower. And don't you wake up the kids." She was right behind him picking up pieces of clothing he was dropping along his way. Once in the bedroom, behind closed doors, Joey's playful mood turned into a barrage of questions.

"How does Mike Keys even know you?" he asked her.

"I don't know. It's a small world. People talk. If you'd tell me what was said then I could at least defend myself."

"Do you feel like you need to defend yourself?"

"No. But, I don't even know what he said that has made you so angry."

"Well, as soon as you decide to tell me how the two of you know each other, I'll be happy to tell you what he said. Now, would you like to put something on this cut for me?" he asked, pointing to the corner of his eye.

"I will if you'll go take a shower first," she said and flopped down on the bed. Joey did as he was told. Laura was laying on the bed when it dawned on her, oh no, the caller ID. She made sure that the shower was still running, then she tiptoed down the stairs and listened to Mark's breathing. Yea, he's asleep, she thought. So she made her way to the kitchen where she saw the red light on her caller ID and quickly deleted Mike's number.

"Are you listening to me?" Joey said from behind the bathroom door as Laura quietly entered the bedroom.

"What? I didn't hear you," she answered, as she resumed her position on the bed.

"Hell, forget it," he said, coming out of the bathroom. "We'll talk about it tomorrow."

# Chapter 22

When Joey went downstairs the next morning, Mark had already gone home but he'd left Emily there, knowing that Laura would wake her up and get her ready for daycare while she was getting her own boys ready for school. And that, she did. But this morning Laura couldn't wait to go to Gail's house. She just had to tell her about everything that happened last night. Well, everything, that is, except the part about Mike Keys.

And much to her surprise, when she arrived at Gail and Larry's, Mark and Joey were already there and seated at the breakfast table. They were all talking and laughing about last night's ordeal. "Come on in and fix yourself a plate," Larry said to her. Then he said to Mark, "How'd you come out lookin' so good? Joey's got twice as many battle scars as you do."

"Because I learned how to cover my face," he said sporting only a few cuts and bruises.

"Why, this is a shiner any man would be proud to wear," Joey laughed. "But," he said reaching over to poke Mark in the ribs, "if I had a face like that, I'd cover it up too. It can't take much more damage."

"I don't think it is funny at all," Gail said interrupting their fun.

"I don't either," said Laura.

"You two are acting like a couple of hoodlums," Gail added.

"And I know I raised you to know better than that."

"Aw now Gail, lighten up," Larry told her. "It's not like they go around picking fights. They were just defending their wives' honor. Probably did 'em good to let off a little steam. And, well, it sounds to me like the other boys needed their butts whipped. They had no business talking that trash."

Laura still didn't know what had been said, but she listened to Gail and Larry go at it and didn't dare ask. Maybe she would ask Gail after the guys left for the barn.

"They're acting just like you," Gail told him. "They should have just walked away, but they've got too much Lake in them to try to avoid trouble."

"Oh and some great role model you've been for them lately."

"Yea, Mom," Joey broke in. "I found out that you got Laura an appointment with your shrink and you didn't even ask me about it."

"I didn't know I had to ask you." Then, with chin aquiver, "I was just trying to help."

"Well, don't be so much help, Mom. You've got enough problems in your own marriage to work on, without trying to fix mine."

The room was suddenly silent. No one even looked at anyone else. Then finally Mark said, "I'm going to the barn. Thanks for breakfast." Larry and Joey were right behind him.

They hadn't been at the barn long when Sam showed up. "Larry," he said, "don't you think it'd be a good idea if Mark and Joey went to see Marty today and paid for any damages their little adventure might have caused."

"I sure do Pop. If they're gonna play, then they're gonna have to pay," Larry said with a wink.

"I don't think that there'll be many more adventures on my part," said Joey. "I'm so stove up I can't hardly move. I guess I'm just gettin' old."

"Horseshit, boy," Sam said. "You don't know nothin' about gettin' old. Why, I'm so old, when I go outside for a walk, the buzzards start to circle."

They all busted out laughing and Joey grabbed his stomach in pain. "Damn. Don't make me laugh."

"What's the matter?" Mark asked. "Can't take it?"

One thousand miles away, Hunter picked up the phone to make flight arrangements back to Kentucky. He was anxious to get back home and out of the heat. The island wasn't that big and if there was anything else to be discovered, he would have done so by now. John and he went to every nightspot on the waterfront, not to mention a few others, and no one knew a thing. Several people recognized Jason's picture, and one girl told Hunter that Jason Kelley promised her he was coming back to get her. But, she had not heard from him since he'd left the island. He gave John a number where he could be reached and John promised he would call if Jason showed up.

In the miner's shack, Kelley thought of his son's birthday and another night spent chained to the floor. He was beginning to lose all hope of ever seeing his kids again, and feelings of desperation were getting harder and harder to shake off. Since Larry had asked him what he'd heard when Lyn's car crashed, he'd found it almost impossible to sleep. "How could she have been so stupid?" he asked himself. "How could she have let Mark find out about them?"

He remembered how they'd argued over that very thing the day of the wreck, although his memory was becoming more and more distorted from lack of sleep. His sleep deprivation was not only taking a toll on his mental state, but on his physical condition as well. His movements had slowed and his stooped posture was much like that of an eighty-year-old man. His back hurt terribly and he was extremely weak. Even though Larry always brought him plenty of food and water, he was no longer hungry. He knew he needed to eat to keep up his strength, but the knots in his stomach made food seem nauseating.

Kelley had never been a person to enjoy time alone. In fact, he tried hard to make sure he wasn't, that he was always surrounded by other people and a lot of activity. The anxiety he felt over what was happening to him now and the dread of what would happen next was driving him out of his mind.

He closed his eyes and saw his father standing over him shaking his head disapprovingly. He opened his eyes, rubbed them, and then scratched his scraggly face. Hallucinations were becoming more frequent. Slowly, he stood and paced back and forth across the floor, dragging his chain every step of the way. "I can't take much more of this," he thought. "Maybe I should just go ahead and end it myself. They're going to kill me anyway. Why should I torture myself by waiting? I wonder if I'll be missed. It's not like I've done much during my lifetime. Maybe the kids will miss me. Of course, I couldn't really blame them if they didn't. Adriane will find someone else who'll take care of her. She'll remarry, then the boys will have a father. They'll probably call him daddy."

# Chapter 23

Sunday morning Mark drove toward Louisville to see Elizabeth. Gail had agreed to keep Emily even without asking Mark her usual twenty questions. She realized that he needed to get away for a while. Mark felt that he could talk to Elizabeth without anything being expected of him, and he liked that. She never pressured him to talk, or asked him anything. Well, except during the call he'd made to her last night. But all she asked him then was, "Will you be here in time for lunch?"

When Elizabeth opened the door, Mark could smell the delicious lunch that she'd prepared. "Something smells good," he said, after giving her a big hug.

"It's just a little snack. You need to keep your strength up if you're going to be training for the next Rocky movie," she said with a grin.

"You heard?"

"I always talk to mother every Saturday morning. Daddy told her and, of course, she told me. You don't look too bad though. You must have held your own pretty good."

"I don't look too bad, but you ought to see Joey."

"How is he?"

"Oh, he'll live. But, he's black and blue from head to toe."

They laughed and ate as Mark relived the entire event for her. Mark told her about meeting Kathy, and he wanted to give it enough time to see where it went, but that he wasn't in any hurry. He talked a lot about Emily and voiced his concerns about Gail and Larry.

It was well into the afternoon when, out of the blue, Mark said, "I can still smell her."

"What?" Elizabeth asked.

"Even though I've bought all new stuff and gotten rid of all

Lyn's things, I can still smell her when I walk into my house."

"I think I'll have a beer. Do you want one?" was her only response.

"Yea."

So she fetched them both a beer, loaded the CD player, and swapped their dirty ashtray for a clean one. "You like blues?" she asked sitting back down.

"Yea. She was cheatin' on me. And you know what, even after all this time, I just can't let that go. You know? I mean, was our whole life a lie? Sometimes I think about it until I go numb. I think my brain just shuts down after a while. You know what I mean?"

"Yea," she said. "I've got a few ghosts of my own."

"I don't think it would be so bad if I could have confronted her with it. I feel like she cheated on me and then she cheated me out of an explanation. I think if I could talk to her now, that's all I'd want to know. Why?"

They moved to the den and Elizabeth rearranged herself on the floor and lit another cigarette. "But what if you found out and decided you really didn't want to know after all?"

"Then I guess I'd just have to live with it."

They sat in silence for a while, just listening to the music. Then Elizabeth said, "Do you know what a broken heart sounds like?"

"What?"

"A door slamming and footsteps walking away from it."

"I guess I would describe it like a Jenga tower falling. You know that game where everyone keeps taking blocks away until finally it looses its balance and falls? Yea, that would be it. I feel like people keep pulling parts of me away until, one of these days I'm going to come crashing down."

"Aw yes, but we are taught that if we fall down, we must get right back up. It builds character you know."

"I've got enough character to do me for a lifetime. I wish I could just let it go. I know I need to. And I try but it's hard."

"Maybe you're afraid that if you let go of the bad memories and all of the hurt she caused you, you'll have to let go of the love you still feel for her."

"I don't still love her. I mean, did she ever once show any feelings for what I wanted or for what I might need? How could she have loved me and do what she did? How? Believe me, I stopped loving her the minute I found out she was screwing around on me."

"Well, if that's what you want to believe."

"What's that supposed to mean?"

"It means that, sooner or later, you're going to have to be honest with yourself. Come on Mark, love is not something you can just turn off like a light switch. At least I never could."

Mark sat in silent retrospect for a moment. "Maybe you're right. You got any more beer?"

"Sure. Be right back. Have you given any thought to what you might want to do with the rest of your life?" she asked on her way to the kitchen.

"Believe it or not, I have thought a little bit about going back to school. I haven't gotten real serious about it yet though."

"That'd be great," she said handing him a beer and opening another for herself.

"It might be a way to meet women."

"I swear. You men are all the same."

"Seriously though, I don't like dating. I'm too old to play those silly little high school games and besides that, I've got a kid. Any woman who takes me for the long haul will be getting a package deal. Two for the price of one, you know."

"I don't like it either."

"I feel like I don't really fit in anywhere. I mean, I'm not married, but I don't really feel single either."

"I know it's hard, but try not to dwell on the past so much. You're going to "what-if" yourself to death."

"What?"

"You know. What if this had happened or what if that hadn't

have happened. What if I'd done so and so different? We all do it. But all the what ifs in the world won't change what's already happened. All that'll do is drive you crazy. You've got to press forward. Figure out what you want to do with the rest of your life and go to doing it, right now, today. This is where you are and this is where you've got to start from."

"I can't get a 'do' over?"

Elizabeth laughed. "I wish we could get do overs, but I probably would have already used up my share. There's a lot of stuff I would have done over."

They talked and ate and laughed and cried until late that night when Mark asked, "Do you mind if I crash on your couch tonight and drive back in the morning? I think I've had way too many beers."

"I think that would be pretty smart. Do I need to wake you at any certain time?" she asked pulling a blanket and pillow out of the hall closet.

"No. I'll wake up early. I always do and I'll just let myself out. And thanks for everything."

"Anytime," she said. "Sleep tight. And be careful driving home in the morning."

Larry laid awake, his mind skipping from one thing to another. He was going to have to do something with Kelley soon. He could not go on like this much longer. No matter how hard he tried to justify his vengeance, the guilt was eating away at him.

His mind went to the sermon in church that morning where the minister discussed Paul's writing to Timothy about the concerns he had with the life of the entire church. He talked about sexual perverts and liars and kidnappers and those who won't tell the truth in court. Brother Patrick had really gotten Larry's attention with the word kidnapper. And when he spoke about teaching people to have genuine love for one another, as well as a good conscience and true faith, Larry felt like crawling under the pew.

Gail knew something was up, although Larry thought her to be too self-absorbed to be very interested. She had awakened him from a dream the night before and asked what he was screaming about. He had told her that he couldn't remember. But, it had been so dreadfully real that he had indeed remembered every detail of it very clearly. Thinking of it now, he shivered and pulled the covers up around him.

He had died. He didn't know how he had died because when his dream began, he was already dead. But he had a vivid memory of a dark, cold room with an ascending staircase in one corner and a descending staircase in the opposite corner. Nothing else was in the room. Larry followed the upward staircase, climbing higher and higher and, as he did, his surroundings became lighter and brighter. When he reached the top of the staircase, the light was very bright, and he remembered a warm wonderful feeling. But the man who came to meet him would not let him through the gates, and told him he must go back down and take the other staircase. "No," Larry had screamed. "I don't want to leave." But the gatekeeper would not take no for an answer, and Larry returned to the room and stopped there to rest, not wanting to go any farther. Suddenly, the upward staircase disappeared right before his eyes. Then the walls began to close in on him until soon the descending staircase was all that remained. He took a quick step down as the top stair vanished. Then another and another as one by one, the stairs faded from under him forcing him downward. They were disappearing faster and faster and Larry lost his balance and fell into the blackness below. And he fell and he fell and he fell.

Something had to be done soon. He would talk with Sam first thing in the morning before he went to check on his hostage. Maybe they could come to some kind of decision. Everything was making him paranoid. And now he was afraid to sleep for fear he would talk out loud and Gail might hear. He wrestled with his conscience until exhaustion triumphed and he drifted off.

Kelley lay on his bed humming the tune to a song, but he could no longer remember its name. He tried to think of the words, but they were nowhere to be found. He stood up and dragged the chain to the center of the room, his head spinning from the slightest physical exertion and his stomach churning from the urinous odor coming from the hole in the other room.

He dropped to his knees and began to pray. "Oh please, God. Please help me," he cried. "I promise to be a good person if you'll just help me out of this mess. I'll be a good father. I'll even be a good husband. Just please, please save me."

# Chapter 24

It was business as usual when Mark went to the barn the next morning, and he fully expected that Joey would have a lot of questions about his trip to Louisville last night. But, Joey never asked him the first thing. In fact, his quietness was so out of character that Mark finally asked him if there was something the matter.

"Something's going on with dad," said Joey. "I don't think it's financial because if it was, he wouldn't be goin' ahead with all of these barn renovations. But, something is definitely bothering him. He's been at Papa Sam's since early this morning."

"Do you think he and Mom are gonna split up?" asked Mark.

"I don't know. I still can't figure out where he's been goin' before he comes to the barn every mornin'. And every time I ask him about it, he just changes the subject."

"Maybe it's just none of your business, Joey."

"Dad has never hid anything from us. Why would he start now? I tell you one thing, though. My curiosity is about to get the best of me."

"Naugh, not you," Mark said sarcastically.

"All right, smart ass. You do what you want. But I'm gonna find out what's goin' on."

"How ya gonna do that?"

"I'm gonna follow him."

"You may find out more than you want to know."

"Then so be it. At least I'll satisfy my curiosity. Come with me."

"I don't know about that."

"Come on, Mark. I've done plenty of stuff for you. I've even got the bruises to prove it."

"Yea, that you have. All right, I'll go with ya. But, if you find out somethin' you don't wanna know, don't say I didn't warn ya."

They watched Larry's truck from the barn and sure enough, it wasn't very long until Larry left his father's and drove in the opposite direction of the barn. The boys jumped in Joey's truck and took off behind him, being sure to stay far enough back that Larry wouldn't spot them.

"He's headed back toward the old coal mine," Joey said. "What in hell could he be doing back there?"

"Maybe he's got a whiskey still set up," Mark said laughing.

"Laugh all you want, but the road looks like it's been seeing a lot of action lately."

"It does, doesn't it," Mark's own curiosity beginning to peak.

Larry had the eerie feeling that someone was following him. He looked in the rear view mirror thinking it was just his imagination playing tricks on him again. He eased his truck down the narrow road until he reached the end where he pulled the truck up into the brush. Looking over his shoulder, he got out of the truck and made his way to the miner's shack.

"We're about to run out of road," said Joey.

"Stop here," Mark insisted. "Let's walk the rest of the way." Mark walked in one of the truck's ruts and Joey walked in the other until they spotted Larry's truck. Then they took to the woods walking through the deeper brush so Larry would not find their tracks, but close enough that they could still see his. And they lead right up to the miner's shack.

"Let's get a closer look," Joey whispered. They crouched down and circled around the shack and approached it from the rear. They could hear voices coming from inside the shack now, so they moved even closer and peeked through the window.

"Shit," Joey gasped. "Is that who I think it is?"

Mark couldn't say a word. His knees felt weak and he shifted his weight, stepping on a dead branch. It snapped in half with a loud pop unable to support him. He stared blankly through the window at the man chained to the floor, unaware that Larry heard the noise outside. "You might as well come on in," he said to the boys.

Mark and Joey crunched their way through the dead brush and snow until they came to the door and went in. They stood soberly in front of their father waiting for an explanation. But Larry addressed Kelley instead. "It won't be long now, Mr. Kelley, and this awful ordeal will all be over with." Then he turned to his sons and said, "Go back to the barn. I'll see you there shortly."

"But, Dad," Joey exclaimed. "What in the . . . "

"Go to the barn," Larry barked. "This is not the time or place to discuss it."

The boys made it back to the truck before either one of them said a word. "Are you all right?" Joey asked Mark.

"Yes. I'm fine. And I'm glad we came. But, I'm anxious to talk to Dad. And I'm even more anxious to talk to Kelley."

"Harry," Sam said into the phone. "This is Sam Lake down here in Lakeland. How're you doing up there in the big city?" Harville Woods, known to Sam and most other people around Lakeland as Harry, had lobbied in Washington for Kentucky's mining rights and later moved there to take a position with the office of the United States Organization of Coal Mining. More importantly, he had recently accepted an appointment as Chairman of the Safety Division.

"It's been a long time, Sam. How in the world are you?"

"Fine, fine," Sam answered.

"Now, I know this is not a personal call, Sam. So, tell me. What can I do for you?"

"You're right, Harry. I do need just a little something."

"Just name it," said Harry. "I probably wouldn't be where I am today if it weren't for folks like you."

"Well then, I'll get right to the point. When the mining company pulled out of the mine that's back here on my place, they left an awful big hole in the ground. I know they're supposed to leave property the way they find it, and well, I've never said anything until now, but it sure would be nice if I could get you to close her up. You see I've got grandchildren and great grandchildren and I don't want 'em gettin' over on the backside of the place and gettin' off into that old mine and gettin' lost or hurt. You know where I'm comin' from."

"I certainly do Sam. I had no idea that hadn't been taken care of. That could mean a heavy-duty fine for somebody."

"Now Harry, I don't want to cause any trouble. Nobody's been hurt. I'd just like it taken care of before someone is."

"I understand Sam. I'll send someone out immediately to take care of it for you. And please accept my apologies for this oversight, on behalf of the entire Safety Division."

"I really do appreciate it Harry, and come to see us if you're ever down our way."

Laura sat at the computer staring at the monitor, her mind going back to the phone call she'd gotten a few nights before. Joey could never find out about Mike. He could never find out what Lyn and she had really done on those weekend shopping trips.

It had all started so innocently. Lyn had talked her into going to Lexington to do some shopping one Saturday afternoon. After they shopped a while, they met Jason Kelley for a drink. This was not the first time Lyn used shopping with Laura as her alibi, but this particular afternoon a handsome young cowboy had come into the bar and immediately caught Laura's attention. After much coaxing from Lyn, she finally introduced herself by sending a drink over to his table.

Mike Keys was unattached and equally attracted to Laura. That afternoon had rapidly turned to evening and a quick phone call home to explain a moonlight madness sale was excuse enough to satisfy Joey. The band struck up and Laura and Mike danced every song alongside Lyn and Jason. They partied until almost midnight, the time that Laura told Joey that the stores would be closing. But when it was time to say good night, Mike would not let Laura leave without her promising that she would see him again.

She'd had a taste of the excitement Lyn kept telling her about. They talked all the way home about the fun they'd had. Laura was captivated by the attention Mike paid her and Lyn had successfully manipulated the security of her secret.

In the next few months, Laura secretly rendezvoused with Mike as often as she could. And Lyn covered for her. They always used each other as scapegoats, being sure to check with the other to make sure their stories were the same.

But now, after Lyn's death, Laura was taking a long hard look at the type of friend that Lyn pretended to be. Laura was ashamed of what she'd done, and decided that she wouldn't be afraid of what Joey would do if he suddenly found out about her cheating. But, she thought, there's no way he can find out. Mike's not going to tell, and the only other person that knows about Mike is Jason Kelley.

She was shivering with fear and thinking of the night she ran over Kelley. She had no idea of what Larry had done with his body. And she knew better than to ask. Suddenly Laura felt very old. Too much had happened during the last year, and most of them were things that she could never speak of again. And some how, she had to find a way to put all of it out of her mind.

"Do you need some help?" Gail asked as she walked past the office and noticed Laura sitting motionless.

"No. I'm okay. I was just daydreaming. I'm almost finished with these statistics for the sales brochures you asked me to key in. Will you help me check them when I've finished?"

"Sure. And then we can talk about buying new dresses for the pre-sale charity ball."

"Oh, do I get to go this year?" Laura squealed with delight.

"If you're going to learn the thoroughbred business, you need to learn it all," Gail said with a smile.

"Oh, I just can't believe it. You're the greatest Gail! I'll hurry up and finish."

The pre-sale charity ball was the most distinguished event of the year. Everyone who was anyone would be there. Laura had heard stories of how a much younger Sam and Martha would stroll to the dance floor when the band struck up with every eye in the room on them. The handsome young couple would dance the ball room dances with such style and grace, that at least half the attendees would stop what they were doing just to watch the two of them. Then slowly, a few couples at a time would join them, until everyone in the room was dancing and having a wonderful time.

Sam's legs wouldn't allow him to dance anymore, but he and Martha still played a leading role in the event, making sure that everyone else had a good time. And when Martha entered the room, all the women still oohed and aahed with amazement and envy. She flew to New York every year, just to have a ball gown designed just to her liking. Laura saw the gown that Martha wore to last year's ball and was so impressed with its elegance, she truly understood what Gail meant when she said that a lot of women showed up just to see what Martha would be wearing.

Laura remembered that ball gown vividly. The strapless bodice was such a deep purple, it was almost black, and it was made of only the finest silk. Being a woman of Martha's age and good taste, she had covered her shoulders with translucent sleeves, just a shade lighter than the dress. The full skirt was ornamented at the bottom with antique lace and one-of-a-kind beading that peeked out from under a translucent overskirt, which matched the sleeves. A coordinating translucent wrap was draped across the front of the dress and over the shoulders to hang down the entire length of its back and flow behind her as she moved about the room.

Even at her age, Martha still had more class than anyone Laura had ever known. Well, this year it's going to be me all eyes are focused on, Laura thought. She could not believe she was going to be included in the social event of the season. Maybe things were about to get better.

Damn Mike Keys. The last thing she needed right now was for him to call. But in spite of the way she felt, and everything that had happened, she had to admit that when she heard his voice, her heart skipped a beat. And the powerful memories of the passion they had once shared invaded her thoughts and proceeded to cloud her judgment more than she realized.

# Chapter 25

Larry met Mark and Joey at the barn, just as he'd promised. He was finally ready to furnish his boys with the explanation they expected, and deserved. Larry then gave his sons a detailed account of Jason Kelley's abduction. Then he told them the reason that he'd concealed Kelley's whereabouts.

"No wonder Laura was acting so weird on New Years Eve," Joey said. "She thinks she killed him."

"She thinks that I picked up his dead body and disposed of it," Larry said, "and I never told her any different. I told her to go on to the park and forget it ever happened. And as far as I know, she's never mentioned it again. But, I couldn't take the chance that Kelley might have recognized her. I didn't want him to give this family any more trouble than he already has."

"It's okay Dad," said Joey. "But what do we do now?"

"Papa Sam has connections. He said he just needs a few days to line things up."

Mark finally spoke, "You tell Papa Sam to take his time. I have a few things I'd like to say to Kelley first."

"I didn't want to involve you boys. And if you hadn't been so damned curious, I wouldn't have."

"I'm glad I know, Dad," Mark said. "And I'm goin' back up there. I did as you told me and I came home and waited for you to tell me what the deal was. But, now I know and I'm goin' back up there and I'm finally gonna get some answers to my questions."

"I'm goin' with you," said Joey.

"Don't do anything you'll regret," Larry said.

"Don't worry Dad. I'm not gonna kill him. I just want to make him think I am. I want to make him squirm just like he made me squirm for months. I'm gonna mess with his head until he thinks he's losing his mind. Just like he made me think I was losing mine." He walked toward the truck, then turned and added, "I'll make him regret the day he ever moved to Lakeland."

"Slow down man," Joey said, as Mark spun the truck around. "Just slow down. We've got to think clear Mark."

"I am thinking clear. I'm thinking clearer now than I have in months."

"Please don't kill me," Jason blurted as Mark and Joey barged through the door. "I never meant for any of this to happen."

"Well what the hell did you think would happen if you kept screwing around with other people's wives?" asked Mark.

"Larry has it all wrong. I never fooled around with Lyn. She tried to get me to but I told her no. You've got to believe me. You're seeking revenge from an innocent man."

"Revenge is such a nasty word," Joey said.

"Please. I'm begging you. I have two sons of my own. What will they do without a father?"

"I guess you should have spent more time with them when you had the chance," said Mark. "And less time trying to keep my wife away from her family."

"What do you want from me?" asked Kelley.

"I want answers," Mark barked. "I've wanted answers for a long time."

"What is it you want to know?"

"Did you love her?"

"What the hell does love have to do with anything?"

"I want to know. Did you?"

"I love my children. Lyn was just for fun. You know. Haven't you ever just needed to have a little fun?" he chuckled.

Joey leaned toward Kelley, and with one hand, grabbed his shirt collar and lifted him off the bed. "You've got a pretty warped sense of humor," he said.

"Don't hurt me, don't hurt me," Kelley begged.

"Where's your sense of humor now?" asked Mark, as Joey

shoved Kelley back down on the bed. "Did she love you?"

"Lyn wanted whatever it was she didn't have. Don't you know that? You were married to her. I didn't force her to do a thing she didn't want to do. You can do anything you want to me, but that's not going to change what she did. And it's not going to bring her back."

"Shut the hell up," Mark spat as he backhanded Kelley so hard it sent him rolling across the bed and against the wall on the other side. At that moment he could have easily beaten Kelley to death. The fire inside his soul had become a raging inferno over the past six months and he had often thought of what he would do should he ever see Kelley again. This was his chance. But, he backed away slowly and turned to Joey. "We better go back to the barn and see what Dad's got to say."

"Detective Hunter," Adriane said, backing away from the door. "Do come in."

Hunter went into the Kelley's home and sat down on the sofa where she motioned. "Can I get you anything?"

"No thank you. I only have a minute."

"Do you have any news about my husband?" she asked sitting across from him.

"I'm sorry to say, Mrs. Kelley, I don't know a whole lot more than when I was here before."

"You haven't found anything?"

"I've found out a few things, just none of them lead to his whereabouts. Mrs. Kelley, didn't you tell me that your husband never carried cash; that he always used plastic for everything?"

"Yes."

"Well Mrs. Kelley, there's been no action on your husband's credit cards since the night of his disappearance."

"Do you think he's dead? Is that what you came here to tell me?"

"I think that all I can do at this point is to lay low and listen. I've followed every possible lead and turned up nothing."

"What about those people in Key West?"

"I'm sorry, ma'am. There was simply nothing there to find. And, from the phone calls I've made to Raleigh, it would be no different there. Believe me, if anybody around here knows anything, they'll eventually talk. More than likely, they'll end up getting drunk and running their mouth. And when they do, I'll be on top of it."

"So you're telling me there's nothing you can do but wait? That's it? Case closed?"

"No ma'am. A missing person case is never closed until that person is located."

"So what will happen if he's never located?"

"After every possible lead is pursued, the file becomes inactive. It remains open; it's just not considered top priority unless new evidence is introduced to the file. But it is never closed unless the case is solved."

"What am I supposed to tell my children?"

"Look, nobody has given up. We're still working on this. I just wanted to keep you informed of our findings."

"I want to go back to Boston," Adriane snapped.

"I don't think it's a good idea if you leave town just yet, Mrs. Kelley. But, if something doesn't turn up soon, it might be the best thing if you and your children do just that."

"So Gail," said Dr. Miller as he entered the room. "How's that journal that I asked you to keep coming along?"

"I've made a few entries," she answered.

"Would you like to share it with me?"

Gail was not expecting this. "It's kind of personal," she said.

"That's all right if you are not ready to share it with me yet. The idea is to learn to channel your pain into something constructive. It's okay to have the feelings that you do as long as you can control those feelings and not let them control you. Journal entry is one way to help you recognize those feelings and pinpoint their causes so that they don't become so overwhelming. You're actually allowing yourself a certain time everyday to take an inventory of your thoughts. To sort through them, if you will, and learn how to manage them, rather than allowing them to manage you."

"Do you keep a journal?" she asked.

"Yes. I have for years and I recommend that most of my patients do. It's really good therapy for anyone."

"I'll read you my last entry," Gail said feeling a little more at ease. "But I feel really silly."

"Really, Gail. You don't have to read it if you're not comfortable."

"No, I want to. I was looking through some old photographs, and, well, all of these things started going through my mind." And she began to read from her journal. "The day your smile left, my smile left too. I wake up in the morning and all I really want to do is go back to sleep. I find it hard to care about anything now. Nothing really matters. I wonder if it ever will. Yet, I do still have the will to live. At least, I think I do. I do go on. Somehow I get through each day. It's foggy. But I manage to move on, not really going anywhere. Just going through certain motions. Involuntary motions. I exist. I hope to live again one day. Yes, I still have hope for life. Never again as I've once known it, but some kind of life. I want to live again. But for now, life for me is only hope. Yes, hope. I still have hope. I still manage to get out of bed in the mornings. One day I will live again. I want to wake up without this pain. But, if I ever do, will I recognize it?"

Dr. Miller was breathlessly silent for a moment, and then he leaned back into his big burgundy leather chair and began to rock slightly back and forth. "Whose smile are you talking about leaving, Gail's? Lyn's?"

"I thought it was Lyn's at first. But, when I look back, I think my smile left a long time before that wreck."

"What do you mean?"

"I think my life really changed when my boys left home.

You know. Like the empty nest thing or something."

"It's only natural for a mother to be lonely when her children leave the nest. Especially stay at home moms who have devoted their lives to their children for years and then suddenly they are gone. It's an enormous adjustment to make. And it doesn't happen over night."

"I just feel so . . ."

"So what?"

"So unneeded. I feel worthless because no one needs me anymore."

"But to become overinvolved in your children's lives as a means to indulge your own needs is the most selfish thing a parent can do, Gail. Do you understand that?"

"Selfish?"

"You can't live their lives for them. You're very lucky that your boys are so close to home. You get to see them as often as you want to, although this may make it more difficult for you to let go and stop trying to control them."

"Control? I'm not trying to control my children."

"A very smart man once said, the greatest gifts you can give your children are: one, roots, and two, wings."

"I don't try to control my children."

"We're about out of time, Gail. I think you need to think about these things we've discussed and continue with your journal entries. Also, I think you should look into those hobbies we've talked about and make an effort toward involving yourself with something you enjoy outside of your family."

"Is that all?"

"No. That's not all. I also think we are beginning to make some progress here. Now, I'll see you in a couple of weeks and tell Laura I look forward to meeting her on Friday."

# Chapter 26

Mark told Kathy he'd call her Wednesday night to make plans for the weekend, but he'd tried all day to come up with an excuse about why he couldn't see her. He finally told her that Larry needed him around, just in case the workers had any questions regarding the renovations, but he'd make it up to her. Mark hated lying to Kathy, but he certainly couldn't tell her the truth. He needed sleep now, because he had to have a clear head in the morning. But he couldn't stop thinking about his meeting with Papa Sam. And of course, the demise of Jason Kelley.

His anxiety rose with the morning sun. He finished his morning routine, then headed to the barn much earlier than normal. Larry and Joey were already there and nervously awaiting Papa Sam's arrival.

"You know Kelley won't just leave here and forget all about this," Joey said. "The more time that goes by, the worse it's gonna be. You know he'll prosecute. It's either him or us."

"I know," said Larry. "But just cool it until Papa Sam gets here. He'll know what to do." Larry didn't have a clue what the old man was up to but he knew that if anybody could take care of this mess it would be Papa Sam. His guts were tied up in knots. He paced back and forth, biting his fingernails and seeing how far he could spit them as Mark put out one cigarette and immediately lit another.

Sam put on his boots and rubbed his forehead. He'd been up and down all night with a sick headache. It was the time of year his sinuses always bothered him, but nothing he took seemed to dull the pain. He filled his coffee cup and drove out to the barn.

As he pulled up to the entrance, he could see Larry and the boys waiting for him to get out and join them. He slid out of his truck, grabbing his walking cane, and he reached in for his coffee cup when suddenly his headache worsened and he became dizzy. At first, no one noticed Sam's lack of coordination. They thought he'd probably lost his balance, as he so often did. But then Sam dropped his cane, grabbed his head with both hands, and fell to the ground.

"Papa Sam," Mark screamed rushing up the corridor. "Papa Sam. What's wrong?"

Joey and Larry ran to his side. "Talk to me Daddy," Larry said. "Say something." But, Sam could not speak. He stared straight ahead as if they weren't even there and then he closed his eyes.

"Daddy," Larry screamed as he shook his father then listened for breathing sounds. "He's breathing, he's breathing," he shouted with frantic relief. "Call 911. No forget it. It'll take them forever to get here. Help me get him in the truck. I'll take him to the hospital."

"I'm going with you," shouted Mark.

Joey called ahead to let the hospital know they were bringing in Papa Sam. Once they were on the main highway, it only took a few minutes to reach Lakeland General Hospital, where the emergency room staff was running to meet them at the door. Larry laid his father on a gurney, and the doctor on call began his examination. "How long ago did this happen?" the doctor asked.

"Just a few minutes ago," answered Larry. "We were with him when it happened and we brought him right away."

"Good, good," said the doctor as he raised Sam's eyelids and shined a light into each of them. "Time is of the essence in a stroke victim."

"A stroke," a disbelieving Mark echoed.

"That's what I'm guessing," the doctor replied. "But we're going to run some tests to find out for sure," he said over his shoulder as the nurses wheeled Sam down the hall.

Larry and the boys retreated to the waiting room. "I've got

to call Mama," Larry said. "No. Maybe you should just go get her," he said to Joey. "She doesn't need to be driving while she's upset. Would you do that, son?"

"Yea Dad," Joey said placing his hand on Larry's shoulder. "Don't worry. Papa Sam is tough. He'll be all right."

"I know," said Larry.

"I'll be right back with Mama Martha. Do you want me to call Mom?"

"I'll call her and Laura," said Mark.

Larry was sitting in the waiting room by himself when Joey returned with Martha. "Do you know anything yet?" she asked as she walked in to face her son.

"No ma'am. The doctor hasn't come back yet." She said nothing else, but sat down next to him and waited.

Joey sat with them for a minute but couldn't sit still very long. He started pacing up and down the hall outside the waiting room, then stepped outside and found Mark having a cigarette. "What the hell are we gonna do now?" Mark asked him.

"We'll think of something, man. Just be calm. We'll think of something." They sat together quietly for a moment then Joey had to get up and walk again. "You comin' in?" he asked.

"I told Mom I'd wait for her out here."

Joey left Mark sitting outside the emergency room entrance and walked back in the door just in time to see the doctor coming down the hall. "How's Papa Sam?" he asked hurrying to meet him.

The doctor turned into the waiting room with Joey at his heels. "Mrs. Lake?" he asked in Martha's direction.

"Yes, Dr. Voyles," Larry replied looking at the doctor's nametag. "This is my mother, Martha Lake. Now can you please tell us how my father is doing?"

"Mrs. Lake, your husband has suffered a stroke. It was caused by a blood clot that reduced the blood flow to his brain. By getting him here as fast as your son did, we were able to give him a drug called TPA which works by dissolving the blood clots that cause most strokes. If administered soon enough, it has been proven to reduce or prevent the permanent disabilities that a stroke can cause. There is an increased risk of brain hemorrhage with its use, but we believe that in your husband's case, the benefits significantly outweigh the risks. We're also giving him an anticoagulant to prevent any more blood clots from forming. I found in your husband's file that he takes a high blood pressure medication. Is there anything else that he may need that would not be in this file? Any cholesterol lowering drugs or anything like that you can think of?"

"No, there's nothing else," Martha answered. "Dr. Voyles, I'm sure you're doing everything you possibly can for my husband and I thank you for this information, but Sam has used Dr. Dunbar for years. Is there any way we could get in touch with him for a second opinion?"

"Yes ma'am. I've already had one of the nurses' call him and he's on his way."

"I'm sorry," said Martha. "It's not that I don't trust you, I just feel that Dr. Dunbar knows Sam's history so well."

"It's no problem, ma'am. I would feel the same way. I'm just the physician that was on duty when Mr. Lake came in and time is of the utmost importance when it comes to treating a stroke."

"He was up and down all night long with a headache," Martha said. "Could it have been the stroke coming on then?"

"It's likely, but I can't say for sure Mrs. Lake."

"When can I see him?"

"He's in intensive care so you can go in for only a minute," Dr. Voyles cautioned. "These next 72 hours are extremely crucial Mrs. Lake. After that, we'll know more about what kind of recovery we'll be dealing with. And as soon as Dr. Dunbar arrives and goes over your husband's chart, I'm sure he'll come speak with you."

"Thank you," said Martha. She hooked her arm through Larry's arm and they walked toward the intensive care unit. Joey watched them walk down the hall together, then he walked back outside where Gail and Laura had joined Mark from the emergency room parking lot.

"The doctor says the next 72 hours are crucial," Joey told them. "But I know Papa Sam's gonna be all right." They all went inside to wait on Larry and Martha.

"Daddy looks bad," Larry said to Gail, as he and his mother returned to the waiting room. "Do you want to go see him?" he asked Joey.

"Can I?"

"Yea, you and Mark can go back for a minute." Then he spoke to his sons as if to warn them of what they were about to see. "His left side is paralyzed, boys. His face is drawn and his speech is slurred, but he did know who we were. There are a lot of monitors connected to him and the nurses want him to be as still and quiet as possible, so try to discourage him from talking if he tries to." They walked fearfully down the hall and into intensive care.

The minute Sam saw Joey and Mark standing over him he tried to speak. "Sh," Joey said.

"Don't try to talk, Papa Sam," said Mark. "Everything's going to be all right." Mark reached out and held Sam's right hand.

"We're here for you," Joey said. "The nurses won't let us stay back here with you very long because they want you to rest, but we'll be right outside in the waiting room. And we'll come back and see you as often as they'll let us." Sam nodded his head that he understood.

"Don't worry about a thing Papa Sam," said Mark. "We're gonna take care of everything out at the mine. You just lay here and try to get better." Sam made a slow motion for him to lean closer.

He was trying to find the words to tell Mark something when a nurse came in and told the boys they would have to leave. "I'm afraid your visit is up," she said. "Mr. Lake needs his rest."

"I'll be back, Papa Sam. Don't worry. Joey and I will take care of everything. You just get some rest."

"The nurse made us leave," Joey said entering the waiting room where they found Martha instructing Larry on how to get in touch with his brothers. Martha decided to call Elizabeth herself. A real daddy's girl, she would not take the news of her father well.

Then Dr. Dunbar came into the waiting room and sat down across from Martha. "I know that Dr. Voyles has explained Sam's condition to you, Martha. And, I just want to reassure you that everything possible is being done for him. Do you have any questions you'd like to ask me?"

"Dr. Voyles said that Sam wouldn't be out of the woods for at least 72 hours?"

"That's right," said Dr. Dunbar. "We expect there to be some swelling of the brain after a stroke of this nature, which is why we are not giving him anything for pain. How much swelling, we do not know. We have a surgeon out of Lexington on stand by in case the swelling is to the extent that the pressure would need to be relieved, but we feel that it would be better to have the surgeon come here rather than to move Sam right now. You see, the x-rays reveal that when Sam fell, his left hip was broken and a couple of discs in his back were shattered."

"So what you mean," Joey scowled "is that if he lives through the next 72 hours, then you'll worry about fixing his hip and back?"

"Hush Joey," said Martha. "Is this hospital equipped to handle such a surgery should it become necessary?"

"Yes ma'am," answered Dr. Dunbar. Then he continued, turning in Joey's direction, "Sam is too weak to make it through any surgery right now, son. His best chance of survival is to get him through this first critical stage. Then we'll know more about what we are dealing with in the way of his recovery."

"So all we can do is wait?" asked Larry.

"No, Mr. Lake," Dr. Dunbar replied. "I would suggest you

start praying too."

"What about that TPA stuff that Dr. Voyles said he gave Sam?" Martha asked.

"All we can do is hope that it was given in enough time to do some good. We will know that in a few days also. Now, I'm going to be in the hospital for the remainder of the day keeping an eye on Sam. Tonight too, if need be. But my nurses can reach me at any time." Then he reached out and patted Martha on the knee. "Miss Martha," he paused, "does Sam have a living will?"

"Yes. He doesn't want to be kept alive by machines. He's told me that at least a hundred times."

"Could you have someone give a copy of it to one of the nurses?"

"Yes," she said as a tear crept down her cheek.

# Chapter 27

"Mama," Elizabeth said, "why don't you let Michael take you home so you can get a little sleep. You've been up all night and you won't be any good to Daddy if you get all run down. I'll call you if there's any change."

"No. I'm not going anywhere yet. If anything happens, I want to be here. Anyway, I dozed a little last night in between visits."

"Well, at least try to eat something, Mama," Michael added. The Lakes had moved into the intensive care waiting room and some of the ladies from Martha's church group had been by with homemade sausage and biscuits and sweet rolls.

"When are Sammy and Phillip going to get here?" Martha asked.

"They should be here any time now, Mama," said Elizabeth.

"All of the flights out of Dallas were booked solid so they decided to drive."

"I wish the doctor would hurry up and make his rounds and come by to talk to us. It's been over 24 hours and I want to know what's happening to my Sam. I want to know he's going to be all right." Martha laid her head in Elizabeth's lap and they both cried.

"I'm scared too Mama," Elizabeth said stroking her mother's gray hair. "I'm scared too."

"Laura," Gail said softly into the phone. "I hate to ask you to do this with Papa Sam so ill, but I need your help."

"What is it Gail?"

"I need you to take our entries for the horse sale to the printer in Lexington as soon as you get the children to day care. The deadline is today at noon and I've promised Larry I would go back to the hospital with him. Could you please take care of that for me?"

"Sure Gail. I don't mind. Just leave everything laying by the computer and I'll come by and pick it up."

"Thanks a million."

"Don't worry about it. What is the word on Papa Sam this morning?"

"Elizabeth called just a few minutes ago and the doctor had finally been by. There's been no change yet, but he did say that the longer Sam went without any complications, the better his chances were of making it through this."

Laura was glad that Gail wanted her to take the sale entries to the printer. She didn't want to be stuck at that hospital all day. Yesterday had been bad enough. As soon as she dropped off the kids she picked up the folder Gail left for her and was on her way to Lexington.

She made great time until she reached her downtown exit but the slowing traffic didn't spoil her mood. She had not been to downtown Lexington since Lyn's death, and everywhere she looked seemed to bring back memories of the fun they'd shared. She eased her way through the business district until she found the one-way street where the printer was located, and she drove until she spotted a parking place.

"Shit," she said out loud, staring straight ahead. "I'm not believing this." She was parked right in front of a gun and hunting supply store. The kind of business Mike told her he owned. She turned off the car, and pulling out the key, she spotted a small sign in the window. The sign read Key's Gun Shop.

That's okay she thought. I'll just walk right down the street to the printing office and drop this information off and come right back and get in my car and drive away. But her curiosity got the best of her, and as she headed back to her car from the printers, she thought more and more about just dropping by to say hello. No one will ever know, she thought. They're all at the hospital with Papa Sam. And it is almost lunch. Maybe he'd like to grab a bite to eat, just for old time's sake. That would be innocent enough. What could it hurt?

Forgetting all about her afternoon appointment with Dr. Miller, she opened the door to the gun shop and stepped inside. "I'll be right with you," came the voice from behind the counter at the back of the store. It was Mike's voice and Laura's heart jumped into her throat. Just the sound of his voice could make her go weak in the knees.

"I knew you couldn't stay away," he said, turning around to see Laura standing there. "I knew you wanted to see me as much as I wanted to see you."

Elizabeth and Larry returned to the waiting room after visiting with Sam to find Martha gazing out the window. "How did you find your father?" she asked.

"He's awake," Elizabeth said. "But he's in a lot of pain, Mama. His back is hurting and his hip is hurting and he feels like his head is going to explode. I just wish they could do something for him."

"I spent some time alone with him last night. He was thinking very clearly and he knows why they're not giving him anything for pain. You're Daddy told me he doesn't want to die in this hospital. He made me promise that if the doctors see there is nothing they can do for him, that I would take him home so that he can spend his last days in his own bed."

"Oh Mama, don't talk like that."

"Elizabeth, you've got to prepare yourself for what could happen. Your Daddy is one tough cookie, but we have no way of knowing what tomorrow holds. And we owe it to him to see that his wishes are carried out."

"It sounds like you've given up hope."

"I haven't given up hope, honey. I just know that Sam feels very strongly about not being kept alive by machines. He wants to face death with as much dignity as possible."

The two were interrupted as Gail came by delivering messages from the bulletin board by the pay phone. She offered to go home and check the messages there and to bring a change of clothes back for Martha since she knew she would not leave the hospital.

"She seems like she's doing much better," Elizabeth said to her mother as Gail joined Larry and the boys.

"Yes she does. But then, this family has always pulled together in a crisis."

"Where is Laura?" Joey asked Gail.

Sensing his implication she replied "Do yawl never talk any more? I sent her to Lexington to take the sale entries to the printer this morning. And she had an appointment with Dr. Miller this afternoon." Then in a patronizing tone, "Don't worry. I'm sure she'll come by the hospital as soon as she can."

"Why does my mother know more about my wife than I do?" Joey asked Mark in search of an ally. They moseyed over to the coffeepot by the nurse's station, and when out of earshot, Joey asked Mark, "What do you think we ought to do with Kelley?"

"I'm thinkin' on it," Mark said pouring a cup of coffee. "I wish I knew what Papa Sam was trying to tell me when the nurse ran us out. I'm gonna try to find out the next time I'm able to get in to see him." Mark was so dismayed at this point that he left his coffee cup sitting there and wandered out into the hallway where he walked up and down trying to organize his turmoil.

Kelley paced back and forth within the confines of his prison. No one had come to check on him yesterday, and it was now well after noon before Larry arrived. Or maybe it wasn't as late as he thought it was. Something was about to happen. He knew it. The end was drawing near. He could feel it in his gut. The way Larry had come and gone so quickly. He didn't stop to be his usual obnoxious self. I wonder when they'll do it. I wonder how they'll do it. No one is ever going to find me.

Kelley slumped over in the middle of the room and sat down on the floor. He sat there thinking about his children and the life he could have had in Key West, until night fell and he was alone in the dark once again. He thought of Adriane, his trophy for public display, and how she'd wanted them to settle down in one place. His thoughts traveled back to his own childhood, and then to the day that his mother died and how empty he'd felt when he realized that he would never see her again. He tried to concentrate on what she looked like, but it was hard to remember certain details. If anybody does find me, it'll probably be too late.

His body stiffened as it absorbed the coldness through the planks in the floor and Kelley rolled onto his knees and pushed himself up. He straightened his back and stretched his arms, then took a slow, rigid step toward the bed. As he lifted his foot, he heard a subtle creak of the plank as his weight shifted. He rocked his weight back on the creaking board again. Then off, then on again. Then he dropped back down on the floor to frantically paw and jerk at the board.

The darkness was maddening and the moon wouldn't peek out from behind the clouds to offer even a speck of light. Exhaustion came immediately and Kelley tried to convince himself that the solitary confinement was making his mind play tricks on him again. But he wasn't convinced. Instead, he talked himself into waiting until the sun came up to try and dislodge the board. He tried to rest, but his hand found a nail head sticking out of the plank and he scratched at it with his fingernail. He scratched and clawed as fatigue overwhelmed his cold, weakened body and he forgot what it was he needed to do the next morning.

# Chapter 28

It was Saturday morning and Sam had made it through another night with no more swelling. Everyone knew that the longer he made it, without additional difficulties, the better his chances of recovery were, and the entire family's spirits seemed to lift a little now that he'd made it 48 hours. Miss Martha sat at a table talking with her pastor who stopped by to check on things, while the others milled about drinking coffee and talking as they waited on the doctor to update them on Sam's condition.

Larry and his brother, Phillip, watched the clock, anticipating their next visit with their father, and as soon as that time arrived, they headed back to see him. They found Sam still in tremendous pain but his mind seemed to be as sharp as ever. He understood everything that had happened and tried to reassure them that everything was going to be all right. They stayed with him as long as they could then retreated back to the waiting room.

Martha wanted to go back next. She couldn't stand to be away from his side for fear something might happen and she wouldn't be there for him. Tired and weary, she ambled her way down the hall toward the love of her life, unable to imagine what living would be like without him. As she opened the big doors going into intensive care and crossed over the threshold, she looked up to see everyone from the nurses' station rushing to her husband's side. She stopped dead in her tracks, frozen with fear, as Dr. Dunbar ran past her. Then a nurse took her by the arm and helped her back to the waiting room.

Hours passed by before anyone came to tell the family anything. No matter how many times someone would stop a nurse to ask them what was going on, all they would say is, "Dr. Dunbar will be out to talk to you soon."

"I need to be with my Sam," Martha would protest. But the nurses kept insisting that everything possible was being done for him and that the best thing she could do for him now was to allow the doctor plenty of room to work.

Finally, the doctor came to talk with the family and Martha knew from the look on his face that things were not good with her darling Sam. He'd had another stroke, the doctor told them. A massive one, and no, there's nothing else that can be done.

"How long does he have?" she asked.

"It's hard to say. His body is so weak. It could be days or it could be hours."

"Then we'll need to make arrangements to get him home. He doesn't want to die in a hospital."

"Miss Martha, we don't normally move patients on the weekend."

"Whatever do you mean?" she asked the doctor. "If my Sam wants to go home, then I'm taking him home. You'll just have to make an exception. He will not die in this hospital, not if I can help it."

"It's not that simple. He's going to need a hospice nurse. That takes time to set up. We'll also move a hospital bed in for you which will make caring for him much easier."

"You don't seem to understand, Dr. Dunbar. I can well afford a hospice nurse or anything else my husband might need. As for a hospital bed, he wouldn't want it. He wants to die in his own bed. Now start making arrangements. From what you've said, we don't have anytime to waste."

Dr. Dunbar did as he was told, and Sunday morning Sam was discharged from the hospital and taken home by an ambulatory staff that Martha made sure were well compensated for their time and efforts.

Larry took Martha home ahead of the ambulance, so she could prepare Sam's room, and prepare herself for what she was about to face. "I'm gonna help Mama get Daddy settled in at home boys," he told Mark and Joey. "I want yawl to go check on

Kelley."

Kelley scratched through a bag, scavenging for morsels of food like the caged animal that he was. His inability to focus was enhanced by his hunger and now by his anger. Finding nothing to eat, he ripped the empty sack in two and stomped across the floor and back to bed. It was then he heard a familiar squeak and remembered what he needed to do.

In the light of day he could see that the board was beginning to rot, and squatting down for a closer look, he could tell that the only nail holding the one end in place was loosening. He pulled straight up on his chain with several jerking motions, and every time he yanked, the lone nail would rise a little higher.

His body was weak, but for the first time in days, he felt hope. And with that hope he found physical strength he didn't know that he had. He pulled and he heaved at the plank with every ounce of force he could muster. He worked and worked, like a trapped beast willing to chew off its leg for freedom. And finally the plank was high enough to grab the end in his hands. With one big jerk, he pulled the end out of the floor, then pried the other end loose with his foot.

Kelley ran toward the door, carrying the half-rotten board and dragging the chain behind him. He ran toward the bushes, only stopping to look back when he realized the weight of the chain was slowing his getaway. He stopped, caught his breath, and quickly looked around for something to cut the leather strap that connected him to the chain. A sharp rock lay on the ground. Then Kelley crouched behind the bushes and started chopping away at the shackle around his leg.

Mark pulled his truck into the clearing and Joey grabbed the bag of food to carry to Kelley. They walked toward the shack without saying a word. They had both lost enough sleep at the hospital with Papa Sam, and neither of them wanted to look at Kelley. They were certainly in no mental state to decide how he needed to be dealt with.

Kelley hacked his way toward freedom, his attention solely directed on the strap, until finally, with one last whack, he was free. His breathing was labored and his heart beat in his ears as he stood. Then he heard footsteps, and turning in their direction, he saw the Lake boys making their way through the woods heading straight for him.

He stood motionless, realizing that he too had been spotted. He bolted and the chase was on. Like a fox with the hounds on his scent, he tore through the underbrush and ran for everything he was worth. His foot slipped off into a sinkhole covered with leaves and he fell down turning his ankle, but frantically he scrambled back to his feet and ran limping toward the old mine. Joey and Mark darted after him slapping at the tree limbs that kept grabbing at them to slow them down. But Kelley had too great a head start and he reached the opening of the old mine before Joey and Mark could get to him.

Kelley rushed into the man made cave, then stopped and looked around in silent desperation. His heart would not let him run any farther. A lump formed in his throat as his heart beat faster and faster. He could hear Mark and Joey calling to each other in the distance, then he knew he had to press forward, deeper into the ground, so he wouldn't be found.

What Kelley didn't know was, below ground lies a completely different world, a world of secret passageways and hidden dangers. It's a damp, musty world of cryptic tunnels that harbor many terrible secrets from the past. This mine goes straight into the side of the mountain, then tunnels down, falling more than 700 feet, where it branches out into tunnels that honeycomb throughout the mountain for miles. And then, blackness; total and complete blackness!

Kelley went further into the mine, until the ceiling began to narrow. The mineshaft was only four and a half feet tall now, and Kelley had to stoop. But he could still see light from the entranceway, and he didn't need to loose sight of that light. It was his lifeline, his only way of finding the surface. Kelley squinted, adjusting his eyes to the darkness, and followed a broken piece of track that was once used to carry men in and out of the mine. The earth had shifted and the floor was raised; and the steel railings were snapped, as if they'd been toothpicks. Kelley was nauseous. He leaned against the wall of rock and slid his body down to the floor.

He peered at the life giving light in the entranceway, wondering what to do next, and he shivered as he wiped the perspiration of fear from his forehead. He hadn't thought to bring the horse blanket during his frantic flight from the miner's shack. And he didn't have any food or water.

When will the Lake boys give up, he wondered. He wanted out of the mine and wanted the Lakes to leave. He would then be able to follow their tracks out of the area. Oh no, he thought, I wonder how many miners have been in this cave and never left? There'd been many men who'd taken their last breath in this mine's depths. Some had been buried alive by cave-ins and others had been killed as the earth belched explosive gases. Some of these victims were recovered, but others remained entombed for all eternity.

There was only one thing for Kelley to do. He had to wait until Mark and Joey left, until they gave up and went home. Then he would come out of the mine and follow their tracks to the road. Kelley could feel his heart rate slowing now, so he stretched his feet in front of him in a futile attempt at comfort, and waited.

Now, the faint light that once illuminated the entrance to the mine no longer shined in from the outside world. But Kelley still heard the voices from outside echoing off the walls. They must be at the edge of the opening, he thought. Again he waited and held his breath, hoping to understand what the Lake boys were saying, but the echoes off the walls were too distorted and he couldn't understand anything they said.

"I mean it, Mark," Joey said. "A man could go in there and never find his way out."

"I promise I won't go into the mine," Mark assured his brother. "You just take care of Emily. Tell Laura whatever you need to, but I'm not leaving with that son-of-a-bitch still out here. He's probably in the mine, just sittin' around and waitin' on us to leave so he can come out."

Finally, Kelley could hear the voices no more. He stood up as tall as he could, and with one hand on the wall, he scooted his feet in the direction of the entrance. It was deathly dark in the cave, and there was no moonlight to light the entrance. Kelley had never experienced such hellish blackness. He straightened his back, and bit by bit, he crept his way toward the entrance of the shaft. And with each step, the ceiling would rise higher and higher.

Soon he felt a breeze. The air starting to have the fresh smell of freedom and Kelley knew he was almost to the entrance. He shuffled along even faster, the certainty of his escape the only thing on his mind. It can't be far now, he thought, as he stopped for a second to take in a deep breath of the clean air. It was then that he heard a faint clicking noise. He tiptoed closer to the exit, holding his breath and listening intently.

There it was, another click. Then another. And then a red light. He couldn't believe his eyes. There, in the dark, was one of the Lake boys building a fire. He watched in disbelief as the fire grew larger in size and the smoke followed him into the mine. The fire was bright enough now that he could see his opponent leaning against a tree and lighting a cigarette. The smoke lingered in the entrance of the mine and he had to move out of its way to catch his breath.

Damn it, he thought. Kelley knew his physical strength was no match for the young man's outside. The cold, hungry, and exhausted Kelley retreated back into the mine. The ceiling lowered again, and he banged his head against a rock, causing dust and debris to shower down upon him. Kelley sat down rubbing his eyes, only to find the same eerie darkness again when he opened them.

He stared toward the entrance and watched. The rock formations and abandoned machinery seemed to come alive with movement as the firelight danced on the rusting metal. Oh, the stories those machines could tell, if they could talk. He heard a squeaking noise and something ran across his foot. He jumped, banging his head on the rocks again, and scrubbed his feet back and forth across the floor to scare the varmint away. Rats, he thought to himself. This place must be full of rats and bats, and probably no telling what else.

Kelley moved a few feet closer toward the firelight, then he sat back down. Somewhere deep in the darkness, at the rear of the tunnel, a boulder broke loose and dropped from the ceiling, followed by ghastly, screeching noises that filled the blackness. He tried to think of what he would do when he made his way out. Then he made a silent vow that he would not allow his imagination to play tricks on him.

That boy can't stay awake forever, he mused. He began planning the route that he would take whenever his guard drifted off to sleep. But try as he might, it was becoming more and more difficult to focus on one thought. The harder he concentrated, the more his thoughts kept jumping around, first on one thing, and then another. His mind seemed to race in circles, and then he found himself trying to recall just exactly what had gotten him into this mess. Oh yea, he remembered, it was that Lyn girl. He hadn't even cared that much about her. How could she have taken him seriously when he told her they'd run away together? What an idiot, he thought. He'd just wanted to have a little fun. As young and beautiful as she was, she was not sophisticated enough to keep for very long. The thing with her was just supposed to have been a fling, and she had to go and screw it all up.

Kelley gradually grew less aware of the dangers around him as his mental energy weakened. He was losing his ability to reason, and his desire for freedom was now taking a back seat to his need for food and warmth. His lips were parched and cracked.

He began groping the wall with his hand for any seepage of water. The fact that he could smell the moisture, literally feel the dampness in the air but could not drink, was driving him insane. When his hand touched something wet, he pressed his face to the wall and licked the moisture that oozed between the layers of coal and trickled down the side of the cave.

Outside, Mark was also in need of something to drink. He was stranded in the woods without his whiskey, and it was impossible for him to push the memories of Lyn out of his mind. He stared spellbound into the fire, remembering the good times, and struggling to hold on to them. But the flames seemed to summon up too many demons of the past. A log shifted, sending sparks into the air and wafting skyward his memories of the dirty deeds of others.

Mark felt so foolish. How could he not have known what Lyn was up to? Well, he did know. He tried to deny it while she was alive, but he knew. There'd been too many warning signs along the way. If only he'd paid attention to them. If only things could have been different. Now, coyotes were yipping in the distance, as if they were laughing at him and making fun of his willingness to be taken in by Lyn's lies. Mark threw a log on the fire and lit another cigarette.

In the mine, strange moaning and banging sounds were emanating from the rear of the mine as Kelley broke off what he thought to be a piece of coal and hunkered down to suck the moisture from it. Kelley drew his knees to his body, covered his ears, and rocked back and forth, trying to ignore the sounds. He closed his eyes tightly and started to hum. He had to resist his impulse to run from the mine and beg for his life.

Alone by the fire, Mark was forced to take a long, hard look at his decisions of the past, the way he'd acted on impulse. Tonight, he was looking at his marriage with humility and admitting that there were certain things he could have done differently. It was time to stop cheating himself out of his grief. It was time to look at his life and know that, even though his questions would never be answered, he was finally free from a horrible situation. Mark finally admitted that his marriage would only have gotten worse if it had continued.

Maybe Elizabeth had been right. Maybe he did still love her. And in some ways, he probably did. But he'd lived with such a black heart since Lyn's death. The wind whined as it made its way around the rocks at the opening of the mineshaft, interrupting Mark's thoughts only briefly. And now, with Kelley trapped inside the mine, Mark no longer felt like the victim.

At home that evening, Joey tried to act as if things were normal, but as soon as Laura went upstairs to put the children to bed, Joey grabbed the phone and called his dad.

"Let's tell our wives we're going to check on a sick horse. Meet me at the barn," Larry said.

When Joey arrived, Larry was charging his cell phone and gathering flashlights and some other items they might need. They hastily thrashed out their predicament, then packed their gear.

"We gotta make a choice Dad," Joey proclaimed. "It's either him or us."

"I know," said Larry. "Just be calm and let's get out there and check on Mark. If Kelley comes out of that mine, he'll kill him. And he don't need that on his conscience. He's got enough shit to deal with."

It was just before midnight when they reached Mark. They found him squatting by the fire, but he didn't seem like the same man that Joey had left out there just a few hours earlier. Mark was much calmer and was thinking more rationally than when he'd first discovered Kelley's whereabouts. "How's Papa Sam?" he asked as his dad and brother approached the fire.

Larry backed up to the fire to warm. "Things are about the same, but Mama's doing much better now that she knows daddy is getting what he wanted."

"Just think, man," said Joey. "If he hadn't of stopped to take that chain off, he could have been long gone by the time we got here."

"But he wasn't," Larry said, picking up a long stick from the fire and lighting a cigarette with the burning end. "We know where he is, and he's not going to cause any more trouble."

"So what's next?" asked Mark.

"Right now, the best thing to do is wait on daybreak and make sure Kelley doesn't come out of that mine." So they waited and talked about what to do. Then, they argued over who would do it. None of them wanted to be the one to pull the trigger, but each of them knew it was inevitable.

# Chapter 29

Martha sat by Sam's side, holding his hand and talking to him as the sun came up to greet the day. "How's he doing, Mama?" Michael asked, entering the room.

"He's holding on. Here," she said, placing Sam's hand in Michael's. "Talk to him while I find him a blanket. He feels cold." Then shaking her head, "The hospice nurse said that this would happen."

"Have you been out of that chair all night?" he asked.

"Why, certainly not. And don't fuss at me. I'm right where I want to be."

"I wasn't going to fuss at you. I'm where I want to be too. All of us are Mama."

During the next few hours each one of the children visited their daddy. Each one, except for Larry. Sam grew more restless with every passing moment. He pulled angrily at the bedclothes and blurted out something that no one understood, then returned to his unresponsive, comatose-like state.

Elizabeth stroked her father's hair. "It's me, Daddy. Elizabeth. I'm going to put some Vaseline on your lips because they sure are dry. Maybe that will make you more comfortable." She doctored his lips and said, "You used to do that for me when I was a little girl. Remember? And you would put it on my cheeks when they would get so chapped from the wind. I love you Daddy."

Larry paced around the dying fire, and Mark and Joey tried to come up with another solution to their problem when they heard a truck in the distance. "Who in the hell could that be?" asked Larry.

"I'll go see," said Joey, jumping up to take a look. Mark and

Larry scrambled to their feet. "It's two men in a government truck," said Joey, peering through the thicket. "It has United States Organization of Coal Mining written on the door."

"What could they be doing here?" Mark asked his dad.

"I don't know," said Larry. "Help me put out this fire."

The two men unloaded their explosives and carried them toward the mine entrance. "Can I help you gentlemen?" asked Larry when they reached the clearing.

"Well howdy there," one of them said. "We weren't expecting to have company."

"We ain't company mister. We own this land. And I want to know what you coal mining people are doing on it."

"Well sir, all I know is that we received orders to close up this mine shaft. The big guys were pretty upset when they found out that the mining company pulled out without cleanin' up their mess. See here," he said, reaching in his pocket and pulling out a work order and handing it to Larry.

"Oh, okay. Yea. My dad did say something about it."

"How's the huntin' been this year?" the man asked, as he and his partner went about setting up for the task at hand.

"Haven't been able to do much huntin' this year. My boys and I come out here and camp sometimes. Gets us out of the house, you know."

"Yep, I know what you mean."

"Can we do anything to help?" an overzealous Joey asked.

"Just get ready to back up and take cover. It won't take long and we'll be on our way and out of yawl's hair."

Mark could not believe what he was seeing. "Papa Sam thinks of everything, don't he," he said to his father as they took cover.

"Yea son. I told ya he'd take care of it."

"Fire in the hole," the man yelled. The blast was so loud you could hear it all the way to Lakeland.

Kelley's body started to tremble as the earth quaked under him and his thoughts flashed back to Lyn and to the argument they'd had on the day she died.

"Hi Jason. Thought I'd call to make sure you were at the office waiting for me."

"Where are you, babe?"

"I'm in the car and on my way to see you."

"Lyn, Mike is in my office. He's saying that Laura won't see him tonight, and he wants you to talk Laura into meeting him. And, he says that if you won't talk her into meeting him, he'll call Mark and tell him about us."

"But Laura is getting scared that Joey will to find out."

"Well, I can't afford for Mark to find out about us. I've already lost one job because I had an affair. I don't need any more trouble. I guess you and I should call it quits too. Don't come to the office, because I won't be waiting for you."

"Don't do this. Mark will never find out about us," Lyn screamed into the phone the very moment her car swerved out of control.

The cave floor rumbled and pushed its way upward to meet the ceiling. Kelley covered his head, like so many miners before him, as the quarry walls cracked and the dirt and rock came crashing down. The mountain showed no pity as it vibrated violently and surrendered to the explosives. And with his last breath, Lyn's screams echoed in Kelley's ears as the rubble pelted down upon him and stoned its prey.

Mark, too, thought of Lyn as the dust began to settle outside the mine. He stood in silence with his father and brother as they watched the entrance to the old mine collapse. In his mind, Mark was comparing the dirt that covered his wife's lifeless body to the billowing dust now emanating from the cave where Kelley's lifeless body lay.

Without a word, Mark turned his back to the unmarked grave. He knew that no one would ever know what happened. He could go on with his life, leaving his past buried, along with Jason Kelley.

Mark had to see Papa Sam now, to tell him what happened,

but he had to hurry before it was too late. All three jumped into Larry's truck and rushed to Martha's. "Where is your father?" Gail asked, as Mark and Joey came in the front door.

"He's right behind us," Joey said over his shoulder, as they ran up the staircase to see their Papa Sam. They walked in the room and stopped to speak to Martha who seemed to be tormented by the waiting.

"His breathing is so labored and difficult," she said. "I hold my breath every time there's a pause in his. I just don't know how he's holding on." Larry caught up to them and stopped to give his mother a big hug. Then everyone backed away so the three could say their good-byes.

Mark took Papa Sam's hand, as Larry and Joey walked around to the other side of the bed. Joey held his other hand and Larry leaned close to his father's ear and whispered, "Every thing is all right Daddy. The mine has been closed up and Kelley was in it. Mark is fine, and Joey is fine, and I'm fine, Daddy. They're here with me, Daddy, and we all love you."

"Thank you for taking care of us," Joey said.

Mark took his Papa Sam's cold, waxy hand and placed it on his cheek. "I'm gonna be all right now, Papa Sam. You've made everything all right again."

A faint smile appeared on Sam's lips, and then he stopped breathing. His jaw relaxed and his mouth opened slightly. The pain line disappeared from his forehead and he was finally at peace.